HATE THAT I LOVE YOU

CASTILLE HOTEL SERIES PREQUEL

ALEXIS WINTER

A wonderful thank you to my amazing readers for continuing to support my dream of bringing sexy, naughty, delicious little morsels of fun in the form of romance novels.

A special thank you to my amazing editor Michele Davine who I would be COMPLETELY lost without!

Thank you to my fantastic cover designer Sarah Kil who always brings my visions to life in the most outstanding ways.

And lastly, to my ARC team and beta readers, you are wonderful and I couldn't do this without you.

XoXo,
Alexis

TEN YEARS AGO I GAVE MY VIRGINITY TO AN ARROGANT SEX GOD WHO NEVER CALLED ME BACK.

Ten minutes ago I just found out he's my new coworker.

Who knew a failed blind date would land me square in the lap of the gorgeous bastard that cut and run after one passionate night ten years ago.

Falling for Nate Baldwin in college was the biggest mistake of my life. Nothing like a good old fashioned heartbreak to teach a girl a valuable lesson.

Now?
He's just a cocky, prank playing bastard in an expensive suit.
I can't decide if I want to punch him in his perfect mouth or kiss it.

Turns out there's a very fine line between hatred and desire.
A good anger bang on a desk…or stairwell…or car never hurt anyone.

But what happens when he calls a truce and starts playing nice?
Not a chance in hell I'm falling for him again.
That mistake stays in the past.

PROLOGUE

TEN YEARS EARLIER...

"Elise! Come on, we're going to be late!"

I continue fluffing up my hair and straighten my dress in the floor-length mirror of my door room.

"Did you hear me? I said we're going to be la—wow!" My roommate Tessa's mouth hangs open as she steps into my room.

"Is it too much?" I look myself over again, a little more nervously this time.

"No! No, not at all; you look smoking! Let me guess...Nate is going to be at the party?" She leans against my door frame with a huge grin on her face.

"Maybe...I tried to subtly ask him, and he said he might stop by. Am I desperate?" I chew on my bottom lip thinking about Nate Baldwin. I've been in love with him since the moment I laid eyes on him at the beginning of the year.

"No, sweetie, you've been in love with him all year. I say go for it. It's kind of your last chance since he's a senior and graduation is only a few short days away. And trust me, in that outfit, he'll be eating out of the palm of your hand."

The hot pink dress hugs my curves like a glove, and the color pops against my tan skin. I usually wasn't so self-conscious about showing

1

off my curves and my long, shapely legs but knowing Nate might be there to take it all in has me checking over every inch and second-guessing my choice. I slick on a matching pink gloss and add a few more coats of mascara to make my green eyes pop. After I slip on my strappy gold heels and grab my clutch, I run downstairs to join the rest of my friends and head off to one of the end-of-the-year frat parties.

I squeeze my way through the crowds of students bumping and grinding to the loud music that thumps throughout the house, stopping to say hello to a few friends here and there but mostly keeping an eye out for Nate. He's hard to miss: tall, dirty-blond, athletic build. He's usually surrounded by a small crowd of women all vying for his attention and that of other popular guys, namely his best friend Vincent Crawford.

Nate and I don't run in the same circles; we met because he needed to fill a few law credits and opted into the same tax law class as me. As a prelaw major, it was one of my core classes, and because I'd spent the summer between high school and college taking every possible dual credit class I could, I was able to start out with some upperclassman classes. I had found out through small talk that he was a business major with a focus in finance.

I wasn't exactly outgoing; I was more of a bookworm, but the moment I saw Nate, something came over me. I turned into a freaking chatterbox reminiscent of a sixteen-year-old high schooler. He seemed amused, but maybe it was more annoyed; either way, I'd continued to talk to him throughout the semester and had invited him to, or maybe suggested he should stop by the party tonight as a way to celebrate finals being over. He didn't seem too interested but gave me a pity smile and a 'maybe.' For me, it was enough.

As much as I might have annoyed him with my banal banter over the last few months, we'd kind of grown to become friends, or at least friendly. We'd chat outside of class here and there when we bumped into each other, and he'd tell me about parties around town. I had only gone to one but was too nervous to approach him for more than a minute when I actually saw him. Tonight...tonight will different, though. I am going to tell him how I feel.

"Is he here?" Tessa yells in my ear over the music.

"I haven—" I stop mid-sentence as I look over her shoulder to see Nate laughing with a beer in his hand. His head is thrown back and his eyes are squeezed shut in a genuine, gut-wrenching kind of laugh. Tessa looks at me questioningly before turning around to follow my gaze.

"Well? Go talk to him!" She nudges me toward him, but I grab her arm in protest.

"I'm too nervous. I need a drink." We both scurry over to the makeshift bar in the living room, and I quickly grab a shot of whatever the guy behind the bar hands me and down it.

"Another," I sputter. After two more shots and a mixed concoction of god knows what, I straighten my back, flip my hair, and make my way straight towards Nate Baldwin.

THE RAIN PATTERS against my bedroom window as I lay in bed well past noon. A soft knock on my door brings my attention back to reality.

"Elise? Sweetie, you gotta get out of bed. It's been three days." Tessa runs her hand over my hair. "And not to be rude, but you're starting to smell." I smack her hand away as I sit up.

"I just don't get it, Tess. He said he'd call; he said he felt something with me too and that he'd set up a date." I wipe away a stray tear that tumbles down my cheek.

"Well, maybe he still will? I mean, he's probably super busy with graduation stuff and his family is most likely here. Just give it some time."

"I sent him a few texts, and he hasn't responded."

"How many texts, Elise?" I can see the countenance of her face change to disappointment.

"I don't know; just a few. Why?" I suddenly wish I hadn't told her.

Before I can stop her, she reaches over and snatches my Blackberry from my bedside table, opening the messages.

"Oh my god, Elise! You sent him fourteen texts? What were you thinking? No wonder he hasn't called you back; you seem like a freaking psycho!"

I groan and throw my arm over my face, lying back on my pillow. "I know! I don't know what came over me. I just got...pissed off. He acted so into me, and we slept together, an—"

"Whoa, wait. He slept with you and hasn't called in three days? Okay, time to get up and shower, Elise. I'm going to give you tough love now; he's not going to call you back and he's a piece of shit pig, okay? A dude who sleeps with you and doesn't call or text the next day is using you and you need to forget about him."

"Wait, what about all that 'he's probably just busy' stuff you just said?"

"That was before I knew he hit it and quit it, babe. Time for brutal honesty, Elise. I'm sorry."

She pulls me off my bed as I stumble to catch myself. "Hey!" Before I can help it, I burst into tears, covering my face with my hands. "I—I gave him my virginity," I say through broken sobs.

"Oh, sweetie." She pulls me in for a hug and rubs my back. "Trust me, your first time is never good, and in ten years, you won't even remember it, and you certainly won't remember Nate fucking Baldwin. I can promise you that."

1

ELISE

PRESENT DAY

"Tessa..." I close my eyes and take a deep breath. "I don't want to go on another god damn blind date," I say emphatically as I plop down on our couch.

"I swear, it's different this time, Elise. This guy isn't some sad wannabe movie producer that still lives with his mom. This guy is legit. He is the founder of the non-profit I work for. He's suuuper hot, and rich too, which isn't exactly a bad combination."

I let my head fall back against the cushion as I consider the situation. The truth is I hadn't given dating a second thought in the last few years, not since my relationship with Brandon ended. Now that I am living back in Chicago, I guess it couldn't hurt to give another random stranger a chance.

"Fine." Tessa claps wildly with a huge grin on her face. "But let me preface it with saying if he's a dud, I swear this is it. I am done letting you set me up."

"I can agree to that," she says with a nod before hopping up to grab a bottle of wine and some glasses from the kitchen. "Can you believe we're living together again? Freshman roommates, and here we are... full circle," she says, raising her glass.

"Well, this is just temporary. Which, thanks a million, by the way.

After Brandon and I broke up, I knew I needed a change. Frankly, I hated my job, and I'd been wanting to move home to Chicago. I guess it was the catalyst I needed. I really appreciate you letting me crash here until I find my own place and a job."

"How's that going, by the way?"

"Honestly, I haven't jumped in with both feet yet. I have some savings, so I want to take a little time off to figure out what kind of firm I actually want to end up at. I've been thinking a lot about corporate law, actually. I found the classes interesting in law school and dabbled in it a little with my internship. All that to say, come Monday, I will be sending out resumes like a madwoman. In the meantime, tell me more about this mystery guy."

She tucks her legs underneath her as she turns to face me with a look of excitement on her face. "His name is Vincent. He's a few years older than us, like mid-thirties-ish? He owns a luxury hotel chain. Castille Hotels."

"Oh, wow, I stayed at one of those in Mexico before. Very nice! Okay, okay, tell me more." I have to admit, I'm more than a little intrigued. The other guys Tessa has set me up with in the past have been a little subpar, to say the least.

"He's so hot…like SO HOT! If I were into dudes, I would be on him like white on rice, let me tell you." I can't help but laugh; I almost snort my wine out of my nose. "Anyway, he's just a really good guy. As the director of his non-profit, I get to see all the amazing things he does for underprivileged youth and battered women. Trust me, you're going to owe me for this one," she says with a wink.

* * *

IT'S SATURDAY NIGHT, and I'm a little nervous to be going on a date with a random stranger. I had pulled out my phone to Google this guy, but Tessa had made me promise not to. She said that the way the media painted him wasn't always in the best light, and she wanted me to go into this with no preconceived notions.

I opt for a sensible but elegant knee-length emerald green dress that stands out against my rich skin tone and makes my eye color pop. I let my hair fall down my back in long loose curls, with winged eyeliner and a sheer gloss on my lips.

"So? How do I look?" I ask Tessa, spinning around to let her take in my entire outfit.

"Umm…you look sensible." The intonation in her voice tells me she is not impressed.

"Why'd your voice go up like that? And why'd you hesitate?"

"Well, you look like a lawyer, babe," she says with a half grimace on her face.

"Yeah, and? I am a lawyer!" I step in front of the mirror in her bedroom to take another look at my outfit.

"Yeah, I know, and you look like you're going to an interview. Why don't you wear something a little more date-like?"

"You mean slutty? Like my tits hanging out, or my ass, or both? You know that's not my style. I prefer to charm them with my wicked sense of humor and intelligence."

"You mean intimidate them…not charm them." I toss her a glare. "Okay, fine, you win. You do look beautiful. Just have fun and try not to ask the guy a million questions like an interrogation or cross-examination, okay?"

I know she means well, but it kind of gets under my skin when she tells me not to be myself. I know I come on strong and I've been told I'm intimidating more than once. In college, I used to let guys walk all over me; that's one thing law school taught me: stand up for what you believe in because nobody else is going to speak up on your behalf.

"Why don't YOU go out with him?" I say, straightening my dress once more before heading out of the room to meet my Uber.

"I will when he grows a vagina!" she shouts after me, and I can't help but laugh.

The ride to the restaurant is relatively quick. I actually love the place he chose; it's a very high-end French bistro that I've only been to when I was in town on client visits…a little outside my budget. I'm not even sure what he looks like, but I was told to mention his name to the host and he'd show me to the table. As I approach the host stand, it suddenly hits me: I don't even know his last name, *shit!*

"Hello, ma'am, and welcome to Everest; will you be dining with us this evening?"

"Hello, yes, I am supposed to be meeting someone here, but I only know his first name. It's Vincent?" I can feel a slight blush creep up my neck. I feel like a silly teenager out on her first date.

"Ah, yes, ma'am, right this way please." He doesn't miss a beat as he motions with his gloved hand for me to follow him.

As we make our way through the restaurant, I can't help but feel Vincent chose this place to impress me. Since I have dined here before, I know it's high end, but it's a hell of a choice for a first date, especially a blind date.

We approach a small, secluded table in the back and a tall, striking man with dark hair rises from the table. *Wow, Tessa certainly came through this time!*

"Elise Taylor, I presume?" he says, standing and extending a hand towards me.

"Trevor will be waiting on you this evening and will be over short-ly." The host nods at us politely before turning and walking away.

"Pleasure to meet you," I say, taking his hand and noticing his firm grip. He pulls the chair out for me, and I take a seat. I glance at him again; he looks familiar, but I can't place it. He's certainly gorgeous: tall, athletic, dark hair, and striking eyes. The kind of looks that women throw their morals out the window for.

He sits back in his chair and reaches for the wine that's already been poured for us. "So, Elise, tell me about yourself. Tessa wouldn't divulge any secrets. She only said that you were beautiful and smart. She was certainly correct on the beauty; guess we'll have to see about the smart part." A cocky grin spreads across his face.

Ah, okay, so this is how it's going to be. I should have known. A man that looks like this with billions in the bank, of course he's an arrogant son of a bitch.

I take a long sip of my wine before answering. "Well, I'm from Chicago, born and raised. I went away to Dartmouth for undergrad, studied pre-law. That's where I met Tessa; we were room-mates freshman year. Anyway, I went on to law school at Georgetown in DC, and I've been at a firm there ever since. Recently had some changes in my life and decided to come back to Chicago."

"Dartmouth, huh? That's my alma mater as well. Small world. Even if Tessa hadn't told me you are a lawyer, it's written all over your outfit," he says raising his glass to me with a chuckle.

I ignore his comment, but maybe Dartmouth is where I recognize him from. "Oh yeah? What year did you graduate?"

"2003," he says as the waiter approaches. He goes over the specials, and we both settle on the seasonal fish Bouillabaisse.

"That was my freshman year. You do look a little familiar; I'm sure we passed each other on campus."

"I'm sure if I saw a woman like you around campus, you would have remembered me." He can't help but laugh at his comment. I flash a fake smile as I chug my wine; this is going to be a long night. Another strike for Tessa.

Sadly, his asinine comments don't let up, and neither does my drinking. I can feel myself start to loosen up a little too much as the wine goes straight to my brain.

"So, what brings you back to Chicago?" Not wanting to go into my recent breakup, I explain that I was bored and unchallenged at my old firm and wanted a change.

"I'm actually looking to get into corporate law."

"Really?" His eyes light up. "I happen to be looking for new in-house legal counsel. Interested?"

"Yeah, absolutely. I—thank you." I'm not sure what else to say, then I remember I have no clue what this guy actually does besides own a luxury hotel chain. "So, what do you do again? I know you own the Castille Hotel chain and that's about it."

"Didn't do your research, huh? I'll be sure to have my assistant set up an interview with you first thing Monday morning," he says with that annoying chuckle.

I try not to roll my eyes; maybe it's the wine, but his endless snarky comments are getting on my nerves. Maybe I don't want to work for this guy.

"Yes, I am the owner of Castille Hotels. After I graduated, I managed to sweet-talk enough investors into backing me to purchase my flagship location on Michigan Avenue and then brought on my best friend Nate to be the financial brains as CFO, and the rest is history."

Nate? And Vincent? It hits me. "Oh my god, you're Vincent Crawford?"

A look of confusion registers on his face. "Yes, yes I am. Am I missing something here? Did you think you were going on a date with someone else this evening?"

"You…your best friend is Nate? And you guys both went to Dartmouth?" I can see I am completely confusing him at this point, or he thinks I'm completely out of my mind on drugs or something.

"Yes, I am Vincent Crawford," he says, placing his hand on his chest and speaking slowly. "And my best friend who works for me is Nate Baldwin."

Nate fucking Baldwin. I haven't heard that name in ten years. Ten years and homicidal thoughts still pop in my brain when I hear it.

"Thanks for dinner, Vincent. I'll see you Monday morning? Nine work? Great see you then." Before I can even register what I am doing, I grab my clutch, throw my napkin on the table, and jump up before scurrying out of the restaurant.

2

NATE

"I don't understand; she just walked out of the date? No explanation? No emergency?" I lean back in my chair as Vince paces the floor in front of my desk.

"Yeah, it was the weirdest date I've ever been on."

I let out a hearty laugh. "Damn, this might be the first time in history Vincent Crawford has struck out with a lady before the date even finished."

"And actually," he glances at his watch, "she should be arriving here in the next ten minutes."

"Any particular reason why?" I ask, confused.

"Tessa told me she's a hell of an attorney and she said she was looking to get into corporate law."

"Is that you rationalizing the fact that you invited her for an interview just to try to redeem yourself and get in her pants?"

Vince laughed, running his hands through his hair. "While that does seem like something I'd do, no. Since Walter retired, the paralegals have been swamped. I need to hire someone ASAP."

"Well, I would love to meet the woman who turned you down," I say with a huge grin on my face.

"Good, because I want you to sit in on the interview."

Vince and I make our way over to his office just as a tall, gorgeous woman is approaching his executive assistant's desk. Her dark hair is slicked back and tied neatly at the nape of her neck; her black dress is fitted but professional, hugging her curves without giving away too much. She's paired it with black stilettos and simple gold jewelry. The woman has style, that's for sure. My gaze follows her long shapely legs, hesitating briefly on her perky, round ass before settling on her face as she turns around. She's stunning: piercing green eyes and full, pouty lips. Her long eyelashes fan out, accenting her almond-shaped eyes.

"Mr. Crawford, pleasure to see you again." She steps toward him and thrust out her hand.

"You as well, Elise. This is Nate Baldwin, my CFO. He'll be sitting in on the interview today," he says gesturing, toward my direction.

"Pleasure to meet you, Elise." She has an impressive handshake, firm. I'm sure it's something she developed as a woman wanting to establish herself as a serious contender in a male-dominated industry. I try not to let my eyes linger on her mouth, but it's damn hard. She offers me a curt, tight-lipped nod in response.

We make our way into Vincent's office and Elise and I take a set across from his desk. "Mr. Crawford, I first wanted to apologize for running out the other night without explanation. Truth is I was just so excited for this interview that I wanted to get home and prep for it and thank Tess for introducing us."

She sounds genuine, but I call bullshit on her excuse. Who the hell runs out on a date because of an interview on Monday morning? I chuckle audibly to myself, causing her to glance over at me with daggers in her eyes. I'm not sure what I did, but this woman seems to hate me.

We spend the next hour going over her resume, experience, and general small talk. She's an accomplished and driven attorney. More than capable of doing the job here at Castille Hotels. I can't help but get the sense that she's jaded, overachieving to prove a point.

"So, what's the verdict?" I ask, turning to Vince as Elise steps into the elevator.

"I'm going to hire her. She's a bulldog, lots of tenacity, and she certainly didn't put up with your shit either during that interview." He gives me a hard clap on the back.

"Noticed that too, huh? At one point, when I made a joke about being married to the job, I thought she was going to rip my balls off."

"As much as I sound like a pussy, I'm glad that date didn't pan out with us. I couldn't handle a strong-willed woman like that. I like them easy and quiet," Vincent says with a laugh.

I POKE my head into Elise's office, scanning the room, but she's nowhere to be found. Vincent had called her the same day, offering her the job, and she accepted. That was a week ago, and I still haven't stopped by to welcome her. I step into the room, checking out her décor. A large, non-distinct black-and-white painting hangs on the wall to the right of her desk. A small plant sits in the window, and a small framed photo of her and another young woman sits on her desk. I pick it up and study it; it's a photo of her when she was younger. She looks so carefree, a smile spread across her face, her eyes wrinkled in pure joy. She has her arm haphazardly around the other woman's shoulders, and they're both flashing peace signs. I look at the photo a moment longer; a sense of familiarity washes over me when I look at her face.

"Can I help you?" I jolt out of my daydream, turning to see Elise standing in the doorway to her office.

"I came by to officially welcome you and congratulate you on taking the position."

"And that involves going through my private things?" she says, walking over and taking the frame from my hand.

"Uh, no, I apologize. I just got distracted when you weren't in here." She's tense, her back is stiff, and her hands are clasped in front of her at her waist. Her hair is down today; long loose curls frame her face, and her lips look pink and shiny. I glance down at them briefly, imagining what it would be like to run my tongue along the curve of them and then nip them with my teeth.

"If you don't mind, Mr. Baldwin, I need to be getting to work." She gestures towards the door of her office and steps back as I come around her desk.

"Right. Well, again, welcome. I'll have my assistant set up a meeting with you this week. We can go over current contract negotiations, and I'll fill you in on where I need your help. I'll be in touch," I say, tapping the door frame awkwardly before stepping out into the hall.

"I'm sure you will," I hear her mutter under her breath. I stop in my tracks, turning on my heel and walking back into her office.

"What's that supposed to mean?"

"Nothing. Have a good day, Mr. Baldwin," she says, pushing me out and closing her door.

I stand there for a moment, confused as to what just happened. How could someone I just met hate me so much already?

* * *

"Mr. Baldwin, your eleven o'clock appointment is here. Should I send in Miss Taylor?"

"Thanks, Mrs. Swinson; yes, send her in please." I stand, buttoning my suit coat before cracking my neck. Preparing myself to deal with another dose of Elise's attitude.

When she enters my office, I motion for her to take a seat in one of the oversized chairs across from my desk. Her red dress hits just above her knee, accentuating her tanned legs and petite ankles. Her outfits are always professional and sensible, but at the same time, weirdly provocative. The way her blouses lay against her skin so seamlessly, how her dresses hug her curves and show off her tiny waist. Maybe I'm losing my damn mind, but I have a hard time focusing around her, and I hate it. She's rude and uptight, a complete contrast to what I imagine her body would be like under my touch.

"So, Vince tells me we were all at Dartmouth together?" I try to make small talk, but she's not having it.

"Yes. So, I went over the contracts you sent me, and I've high-lighted some areas that could result in loopholes or could be thrown out in court. I've reworded them, removing that liability." She reaches into the folder on her lap and hands me several stacks of paper. "I've also emailed you all this information as well."

Very thorough. I'm not at all surprised. "Are you always this atten-tive to detail, Miss Taylor?" I toss her a charming grin, but she's not amused.

"Yes, as an attorney, that's a huge part of the job. I wouldn't be a very reliable employee if I let stuff like this slip through the cracks, exposing us to severe repercussions."

I don't respond right away; I keep eye contact with her as I drag my thumb across my lower lip; I watch as she swallows. Her eyes drop from mine to what my thumb is doing before she squeezes her knees tighter together and sits up taller. She's affected by me.

"Well, that is certainly something I can agree with. Protecting this company and its interests is tantamount to our success." She nods, and silence hangs between us. I don't have anything else to discuss with her, but I'm not ready to let her get back to work. "Speaking of the company, has anyone given you the full tour yet?" I slap the top of my desk as I stand up.

"Uh, no." I can tell she's scrambling for an excuse to get out of it, but I won't take no for an answer. "I really should get back to my office, I ha—"

"You will. Just leave your things here, and we'll pick them up on the way back."

I take her around, giving her a tour of the corporate office as well as the flagship hotel across the street.

"So you grew up in Chicago?" I again try to make small talk as we ride the elevator back downstairs.

She lets out a long sigh, and I see her roll her eyes out of the corner of my eye. "Yeah, something like that."

"This is probably going to sound really cliché, but have we met before?"

This time, she doesn't try to hide her loud sigh and eye roll.

That's it. I don't know what I did to this holier-than-thou princess, but it ends now! I reach out and slam my hand against the stop button on the elevator, causing it to come to a screeching halt. She jolts forward, catching herself against the doors.

"What the hell, Nate?" She reaches for the button to start it again, but I jump in front of it. The look on her face tells me I have about four seconds before she hauls off and slaps me or screams bloody murder.

"No, I think that's my line. What the hell did I do that requires you to treat me like I'm shit on the bottom of your shoe? I spoke very highly of you after you interviewed here. I've been nothing but cordial, but you seem to think you can't be bothered to waste time with me."

I can see I've struck a nerve. Her hands are balled into fists, and her jaw is clenched in a firm line. "You don't remember me, do you?"

"What?" I rack my brain, trying to remember if I've met her before. I'm drawing a blank.

She crosses her arms over her chest, and I can't help but look down at her ample breasts pushed together. "Tell me, Mr. Baldwin, how did you manage to pass tax law at Dartmouth? Was it perhaps with the help of a pre-law major? Someone who did your homework for you and who you copied off of to keep that 3.50 GPA?"

My mouth goes completely dry. *What the fuck?* "Wait...you're Elise from college? The freshman that I copied off of?"

"Yeah, Elise, the freshman you copied off of. Anything else you might remember about me from college, Nate?" She's tapping her foot with one eyebrow cocked. Clearly there's something else I'm not remembering.

"Should I? Did we ho—" I stop talking immediately, the joking smile on my face faltering. Memories are flooding back to me, memories I am instantly regretting.

"The freshman you hooked up with, promised to call, and then you vanished off the face of the earth. One and the same," she says, circling her face dramatically. "Now that we've had a lovely trip down memory lane, I'd like to get back to work." She slams her hand against the button, and the elevator lurches back to life.

I don't say another word the entire trip back to my office, and neither does she. She barges through my doors, grabs her things, and turns on her heel to leave. At the last second, she stops and turns around to face me like she's about to say something but turns back around and leaves without a word.

I sit at my desk and let out a loud, long sigh. What in the hell just happened? Is she seriously still upset over something happened over a decade ago? Suddenly, it hits me; did she...did she stalk me and get hired here just to get revenge on me? I jump up from my desk and stomp toward her office; I am not done giving her a piece of my mind.

3

ELISE

"Ugh!" I yell, slamming my folder down on my desk. I had promised Tessa I wouldn't let this be an issue when I took the job here. I can still hear her words echoing in my head: *"Elise, I mean it. Do not turn this into some dramatic vendetta and make a complete ass out of you and me. I vouched for you to Vince!"*

I pull out my phone to send her a text but decide against it in the heat of the moment. I just need some time to cool off and let her words sink in. It isn't too late to make things right and just let bygones be bygones.

I swivel my chair around to look out my window; the view overlooks Lake Michigan, and it's a clear day. I close my eyes, willing my stress away, and take a few long, deep breaths. I definitely need to find a local yoga studio; I have a feeling I'm going to need it with this job. My mind feels like it's clearing, and my anxiety has settled down to a much more reasonable level.

I let my mind wander to images of Nate. He's still got that boyish charm he had in college, but now he's all man. Tall and built with a jaw that could cut a diamond, and I'm sure a body that would turn me into a quivering mass of jelly. A body that changed since our night together in college. A body that towered over me in the elevator and filled out his suit like a glove. I had tried not to watch his thumb graze his plump bottom lip, but I couldn't resist. I wanted to replace that thumb with my tongue.

"Where the hell do you get off?" Moment ruined. I swivel back around in my chair to face Nate, who has burst into my office without so much as a knock. So much for my anxiety; my blood pressure just shot back through the roof.

"Excuse me?" I shoot back.

"Are you seriously still mad about some meaningless night from ten years ago? Because you need to get the hell over it!"

It takes everything in my power not to leap over this desk and strangle him right now. Meaningless? Are you fucking kidding me? Of course, I meant nothing to Mr. Big Shot Nate Baldwin. I was just another conquest, a notch in his never-ending belt.

"Actually, Mr. Baldwin, I couldn't care less about that night. In fact, I barely remember it," I lie. I refuse to give him the satisfaction of knowing that he stole my innocence that night…okay, stole might be a stretch since I willingly gave it to him.

"Then what's with the attitude?" he asks, shoving his hands in his pockets.

"Has it ever occurred to you that you're just not as charming as you think you are?"

"Psh," he scoffs. I stand with my arms crossed staring back at him without a word. He mutters something under his breath and walks back out of my office.

I shake my head and sit back down only to be interrupted again by Nate bursting back in through my office door pointing a finger at me and shouting.

"Oh! Oh! I remember! You—you were the girl who sent me like fifty text messages and hit me up on Myspace!"

"Stop waving your finger in my face, and it wasn't fifty messages!" My resolve breaks and I shout back at him.

"That cost me, like, fifty bucks, by the way. Nobody had unlimited texting back then!" He points his finger even harder at me.

"Oh, boohoo; take it out of my check, ass-face!" Not my finest moment. I hate that I stoop to the level of name calling and yelling but I go with it.

"What the hell is going on in here?" Vincent steps in looking between the two of us.

"He started it!" I point toward Nate who has a dumbfounded look on his face.

"I don't give a shit, I'm ending it!"

"She's just a bitter hag that can't get over the fact that I never called her back over a decade ago!"

I can feel my face turn red. I'm sure I look like a god damn tomato right now, but I don't care. Ten years of anger towards Nate fucking Baldwin has reached its breaking point and I'm about to blow.

Vincent looks between the two of us in confusion before throwing his hands up in the air and letting out a load groan. "Look, I don't give a flying fuck what happened between the two of you, but you better work it out, understand? I won't have this yelling bullshit in my office. You're both too god damn old for this shit!" I've only known him a week, but I've never seen him so animated or angry.

He walks towards my door then turns around once again. "I mean it. Work it out."

I turn my fiery gaze back to Nate, who's still standing in my office.

"Did you seriously get a job here to stalk me and enact your revenge or whatever on me?" I want to smack the stupid, smug look off his face right now.

"Do you hear yourself? Get fucking real, Baldwin, and get out of my office." He just shakes his head and swats a hand through the air, muttering something I can't make out under his breath before walking out.

I release my shoulders that feel like they're up by my ears and sit back down in my chair. His accusation wasn't completely wrong...I mean, I did jump at the chance to interview here. I rub my temples, trying to release the tension that had built up. Why am I still so god damn attracted to him? I hate that even when he's shooting off his idiotic mouth, I want to leap across my desk and smash my lips against his.

* * *

"THAT'S IT! I QUIT!" I yell, marching through the front door of Tessa's apartment. I throw my bag on the couch and march straight to the kitchen, grabbing a bottle of wine off the counter. I pop the cork and bring it to my mouth, forgoing a glass.

"God almighty, what happened?" she says, pulling the bottle from my lips as a few drops run down my chin.

I wipe them off unceremoniously with the back of my hand. "He's still a complete festering douchebag asshole! That's what happened." I reach out and grab the bottle again from her.

"Anyone ever tell you, you're a bit overdramatic?" I roll my eyes, leaning against the kitchen island.

"He didn't even remember me, Tess. I reminded him and when he did seem to recognize me, it was because I was the 'freshman who helped him pass tax law.' I just…" I let my words trail off, not even sure what I had wanted to say.

"Sweetie, I'm going to say this again, and I don't mean it to be rude, but it's been ten years. TEN YEARS. We go through this emotional cycle reliving the past every few years."

"I know bu—" Before I can finish, she cuts me off again.

"Let's go over the facts. It's not like you guys were dating, and he wasn't exactly a celibate angel. That man most likely got more ass than a toilet seat in an airport. Plus, you guys had both been drinking that night. Now I'm not excusing his behavior because him telling you that he liked you back and was going to call you and all, that was complete shit. He should have just manned up and made it clear it was a one-night thing."

I let her words sink in. There was a lot of truth in what she was saying, but I could never seem to accept it and let it go.

"I hate…I hate that I'm still so attracted to him." I bury my face in my hands as I admit it.

"Well, coming from a lesbian, he was a tasty dish in college, and if he's anything like Vincent who has aged like a fine wine, then I think it's normal. I meant what I said though, Elise; I had no idea that he

21

worked at the hotel. Vince and I don't talk much about his business or his personal life. I stepped out on a ledge when I asked him about a blind date with you."

"I believe you. I think I'm just still not over the breakup with Brandon and seeing Nate brought a lot of old feelings back. I know it's only been a few months since Brandon ended things with me, but we'd been together so long, I guess I just got comfortable and expected him always to be there." Tess reaches out and rubs my arms before bringing me in for a hug.

"I know, babe. How about you get changed, and we'll celebrate the fact that you made it through your first week of work and cheers to a better, less dysfunctional working relationship with Nate. Oh, and you're not quitting, or I swear I will post that video of you in college when you tried to drunk twerk on the bar top and fell off, destroying all the liquor bottles."

"Great, now I have a hostile home environment too." I laugh. "And I looked hot that night so post away!"

"You were drunk and thought you looked hot; you looked like a worm having a seizure, and your makeup was melting off your face. Go change!" She swats my ass, and I head off to my bedroom.

4

NATE

"So, we going to talk about what happened today or should I let it go?" Vince looks over at me as he sets his beer down on the bar. I run my hands roughly over my face; I was waiting for him to bring it up.

"Turns out I hooked up with Elise in college."

"Of course, you did," Vince says laughing. He and I both weren't exactly a one-woman type of man back in those days, not that he had changed much. We both enjoyed our fair share of ladies in college. Who didn't?

"I don't even remember it, man. Or, I didn't, I should say. She cornered me asking me if I remembered her or some shit. I thought for a minute she looked familiar when I saw a picture of her on her desk from a few years ago, but I would never have connected those dots. How can someone so hot be such a bitch?" I finish my beer and motion to the bartender for another.

"Noticed that too, huh? The hot part, I mean, not the bitch. She seems very....uptight." Vince says the last word slowly to emphasize it.

"Yeah, no kidding. I can see why your date with her wouldn't have gone anywhere. She probably would have made you sign a legal contract or NDA before banging her." We both laugh.

"She helped me in this law class senior year. I don't remember the events of the night, but we hooked up. The one thing I remember vividly now is that she was fucking crazy. She sent me like fifty texts and an email or Myspace or something. Alarms went off in my head with that one."

"Well, whatever unresolved shit is between you two, either resolve it and move on or don't, but do not bring it into work."

I take another long pull of my beer. "No kidding, man. I can't work like that. The tension is unreal. I swear, I can see her plotting my murder in those big green eyes."

"Maybe be the bigger man, Nate. Like you said, it's been ten years, so just send her some flowers; women love gestures like that. And with that, I'm out." He tosses a few twenties on the bar top and waves to the bartender, "Goodnight Jamie."

I finish my beer, letting his suggestion sink in. I'm not a completely heartless bastard; it does bother me that I hurt her and never made it right. God knows it took me years to get over Carrie Felton from sophomore year of high school. The first girl I ever kissed, who then told everyone I tasted like old cheese and asshole. Can't hurt to try to make things right. Come Monday morning, I'll send her flowers and an apology and put this shit behind us once for all.

* * *

It's Monday morning, barely past ten, and it already feels like longest week. I ordered flowers for Elise and made sure to have them delivered to her office this morning. I haven't heard a response yet from her, so I am taking it as a good sign. I am just leaning forward to ping my executive assistant to see if she had heard anything when the large double doors to my office burst open.

My assistant Josie is running after Elise, "You—you can't just go in there!"

"Is this supposed to be funny?" she shouts, waving a small card in my face.

"Josie, it's fine. You can shut the doors, please." I ignore Elise as I addressed my assistant and sit back in my chair. Before I can register what is happening, Elise takes the box in her hands and turns it upside down, dumping the context of what looks like shredded flowers all over my desk.

"Here's what I think of your half-assed and cruel apology, if you can even call it that!"

"What the fuck, Elise?" I slam my hands down on my desk, beyond irate at this point. "What the hell is wrong with you? Is a rabid rat inside your brain chewing away all of the parts that make you act like a rational human being?"

"Dear Elise, here's a lovely bouquet of flowers as an apology for my behavior. I thought it was only appropriate to give you flowers since you so eagerly gave me yours." She throws the card in my face, her chest heaving with every breath.

"It was a joke! You are so god damn uptight; you need to relax. And for the love of all that is good and holy, why can't you forgive me for something so menial that happened so long ago?" I am genuinely exasperated, my hands gesturing wildly as I speak.

"Don't tell me to relax! It might have been menial to you, but it meant everything to me. Maybe virginity doesn't matter to guys, but for a lot of girls, it does!" Her words cause me to pause. *Virginity?*

"Elise, honestly, I didn't know. I just thought the card would make you chuckle; I didn't actually think or know you gave me your virginity that night. I—I'm sorry." I suddenly feel like a complete asshole. My attempt at an apology and a joke had gone completely pear-shaped and made the situation even worse.

"It's too late, Baldwin. Fuck your apology, fuck your flowers, and fuck you. Jump up your own ass!" She spits the words at me with a rigid finger point before turning on her stiletto and wagging her perky little ass out of my office and slamming the door.

"It's fucking war now, Elise!" I shout after her as I look at the pollen and petals littering my desk. "Fuck!"

THE REST of the week isn't much better. Elise's ice-cold stare is around every corner, penetrating me. The worst part is, I swear she's upped her wardrobe game just to drive me crazy. I walk behind her in the corridor, watching the sway of her hips in the electric blue pencil skirt she's wearing. It has an exposed zipper up the thigh that shows just a sliver of her toned, tanned skin when she walks or crosses her legs. I want to rip it from her body and then lick every inch of her.

"Stop staring at my ass, pervert," she says without even turning around.

"What ass?" I say, brushing past her to take a seat in the conference room for our monthly staff meeting. A low blow, but she brings it out of me.

We all take our seats as the meeting commences, Vincent at the head of the table going over our numbers, possible acquisitions, and upcoming projects. Each department head has to present, and when it's my turn, I swivel my chair and stand up, making my way to the front of the room. Just as I'm about to clear the last chair, a heeled foot juts out, catching the toe of my shoe, catapulting me forward as I launch the papers in my hand toward the ceiling.

I catch myself, but not before my pride takes a swift kick to the balls and a chorus of chuckles circulates throughout the room. I stand quickly, gathering my papers with the help of Vincent trying to play it off. I refuse to give her the satisfaction of embarrassment, so I say some snarky comment about my legs still being sore from my crazy workout last night.

She has another thing coming if she thinks I'm going to let her get away with this. I wait until after the meeting when I overhear her talking to another coworker about grabbing lunch together. I've noticed that she always changes into flats at lunch and leaves her heels behind. I wait patiently in the hall as I see her enter her office and emerge a few moments later with her flats on.

"Enjoy your lunch, Elise," I say, flashing her the sweetest, fakest smile I can muster. Like usual, she completely ignores me, brushing past me to catch the elevator. I wait until I see the doors close then I sneak into her office, shutting the door behind me. I check the coat closet, but there are no shoes, then I look under the desk, and there they are. I pull them out; the heel is at least five inches. I have to admit, they make her already perfect ass look even more amazing and her mile-long legs look like they could be on a catwalk.

I sit down on the floor, trying to hide my body with the desk as I open her drawers in search of a tool. "Bingo!" I whisper as I pull out a metal nail file. I put the file against the base of the heel and begin to saw, stopping suddenly when I realize that this is pretty mean. Then I remember the smug look on her face this morning when she tripped me in front of everyone. "Karma's a bitch, sweetheart," I mutter as I saw my way through the heel, leaving it connected just enough not to tip her off. I replace the file and the shoes and slip back to my office.

The rest of the afternoon is a drag. The only thing I'm looking forward to is a red-faced, pissed-off Elise storming through my office doors at any minute. I'm buried in my laptop, going over expense and quarterly business reports, when I hear the somewhat muffled shouts of Elise coming towards my office. I can't help but smile. I know I'm about to get living shit chewed out of my ass, but I know it will be worth it. I immediately burst into laughter as a disheveled-looking Elise comes limping into my office with one broken shoe in her hand and the other still on her foot. Success.

5

ELISE

I burst through Nate's office doors, holding up a finger of silence to his assistant, whose mouth snaps shut at the gesture.

Nate is sitting back in his chair, a low chuckle emerging from his broad chest. "You look pretty damn proud of yourself for a dead man," I say as I hurl the mangled and broken heel at his head. He dodges it only slightly, causing his laugh to halt.

"Jesus, Elise, you don't have to get violent over it!"

I lean across his desk, getting my face as close to his as I can. His eyes drop from mine to look down my somewhat gaping blouse. A huge grin spreads across his face when I catch him; he doesn't care as he takes another long look.

"You know, you wouldn't be half bad to look at if you walked around like that all the time."

I stand up quickly, realizing he isn't worth my anger. "Please elaborate on that for me, Mr. Baldwin. Would I be more sexually appealing to you and the other men in the office if I wore shorter skirts? Maybe a sheer blouse with my tits hanging out?" I slowly unbutton one of the buttons on my blouse, dragging my finger down my cleavage. I can see his Adam's apple bob in his throat as his eyes bounce from my lips to my chest. "Maybe then I'd be one of the women in the lunchroom discussing the size of your manhood, praying and hoping you'd give me a second glance in the hallway."

"Yeah, you wish," is all he can manage to muster as he shifts uncomfortably in his chair. A new idea formulates in my head. How easy it would be to manipulate him using my sexuality...such a cliché.

I hop up on his desk and bend my knee, swinging my leg with the still intact heel up on the desk as I reach down to remove it. I drop it on his desk; it makes a loud thunk as it lands between his hands that are flat against the surface. I slide back off the desk. "Those weren't cheap, Baldwin; I'll send you the bill."

He doesn't say a word as I sashay back out of his office. I don't need to turn around to confirm what I already know; he can't take his eyes off me.

When I get back to my office, I close the door and immediately grab a stack of papers to fan myself. I have no idea how I managed to keep my cool through that exchange. A very overwhelming part of me wanted to continue to crawl across his desk and grab his tie, forcing his lips against mine while I slid down into his lap. I take several large swallows of the ice water on my desk, trying to calm my nerves and ignore the quivering desire between my thighs. "Christ, I need to get a grip."

"SO ARE THE RUMORS TRUE?" Amber, one of the interns, asks another intern, whose name I don't know.

"You know I don't kiss and tell. Especially when it comes to the CFO." She emphasizes the O, exaggerating the shape of her mouth as she nudges the other girl.

That catches my attention. A little pit forms in my stomach at the thought of Nate hooking up with the interns, and a little bit of disgust as well. It's one thing to go after a younger woman, but it isn't cute when you're one of the executives and you're fishing in the still-in-college pool.

"Come on, tell meeeee." She exaggerates the last vowel sound, dragging it out like she's an annoying teenager begging her parents to stay out past curfew. She holds up her hands, a solid foot apart as bimbo number two squeals and swats her hands away.

"You're so baaaad!"

I take a sip of my coffee as I wait for my bagel to pop up out of the toaster. Someone enters the room, and I look up just in time to see Nate walk in, his eyes landing on me.

"And here I thought you ate the souls of lonely, innocent children for breakfast." Both girls look over at us, the one's hands still held up in a gesture of measurement.

"Nope, just the hearts of pathetic, bottom-feeding men." He ignores my comment as he pulls a blender from under the counter and proceeds to fill it with frozen fruits and an electric-green powder. This is his morning routine; I know this because I see him carrying around his stupid green smoothie every morning and my office isn't far from the kitchen, so I hear the whirl of the blender.

"Sorry to disappoint, ladies, but it's more like this," I say inching Amber's hands closer together until they're only a few inches apart. I can see the look of shock on their faces; I don't know if it's over the size or the fact that I'm an authority on Nate Baldwin's dick. Truthfully, I couldn't remember how big he was, that one fact is something I so wish I could remember, but for the sake of my mental health and agony, I'm glad I've forgotten.

Nate watches as I move the girl's hands closer together, and her mouth pops open as her eyes jerk in his direction. He's completely distracted, standing in front of his very full blender. He doesn't even register that he didn't put the lid back on when his finger drops down to the power button and presses it on. The blender roars to life, sending bits of milk and chopped fruits and vegetables all over the ceiling as well as Nate's face and shirt. He scrambles to turn it off, but it's too late: the chunky concoction is dripping off the tip of his nose as the bimbos scurry out of the room laughing.

I stand back with a smile on my face as Nate walks closer to me, slowly removing his tie and unbuttoning his oxford. I move with him until my back hits the wall. He pulls the shirt down his perfectly sculpted shoulder and firm biceps, balling it up and wiping off his face. He plants a hand on either side of my head as he leans in. I want so badly to reach out and touch his abs. I've never seen a man in real life that has an actual eight pack. His skin is pulled taut against his rippling muscles, and his chest expands with each breath.

"You are playing with fire, Miss Taylor. Don't think for one minute that I don't plan on punishing you for this."

I feel like I'm about to melt into an actual puddle, but I play it off. "For what? Pretty sure I had nothing to do with this," I say casually, refusing to let my eyes drop down to his chest. I can feel a bead of nervous sweat run down between my breasts. I just pray it doesn't show through my silk blouse.

"You're lucky I'm not into frigid brunettes." His eyes drop down to my neck, focusing on the dip at the base where my skin moves with my pulse.

This game has gone too far, and I'm completely out of my element. I try to swallow down my nervousness, but it's getting the better of me. I reach out and plant my hands on his chest and push him, but he barely moves. I brush past him with both my middle fingers raised in the air, "You wish, Baldwin."

6

NATE

I stroke myself faster, harder, my breath coming out in jagged intervals as I get myself closer to the edge. I imagine her legs wrapped around my waist, my cock buried in her tight, wet pussy as I make her apologize to me. She's panting, begging, gasping for release, but I won't give it to her, not until I hear my name tumble from those supple lips.

I groan as I cum all over the floor of the shower, resting my head against the wall as the warm water cascades down my body. *Shit!* This marks the third day in a row I started my morning off by beating it to images of Elise fucking Taylor. I finish washing off, then step out of the shower.

It's been this way since the first smart-ass comment that fell from her mouth. Actually, it's been this way since I saw her at her interview. The curve of her ass, those full round breasts that I'd kill to suck on. I can't get her out of my head, but at the same time, I can't deny that I have plotted her murder a few times.

She's the type of woman that always knows exactly what to say at exactly the wrong time. Can't ever let a smartass remark go. A grin pulls at one side of my mouth as I think about her, for as much as she drives me bat-shit crazy, she's also so quick witted, it keeps my head spinning. She's hilarious, beautiful, and wicked smart...a deadly combination. I snap out of it, realizing I might start to like the woman if I give it another thought.

I whip my Audi S7 into the garage and wave to Raymond, the attendant. I round the corner a little fast, tires squealing, when I suddenly slam on the breaks. "What the fuck?" I mumble to myself as I look at the small black and red Fiat parked in my spot. The sign above my parking spot is clearly labeled with a red and white metal sign that reads 'RESERVED FOR NATE BALDWIN, CFO CASTILLE HOTELS.' I angrily pull around until I find a regular empty spot and grab my suit coat and a pen and napkin before marching back over to where I should be parked.

I glance at the car again as if staring at it will help me recognize who the owner might be. I pull the napkin out of my hand and scribble a note on it.

Dear Fiat owner, in case you missed the clearly marked sign above this parking spot, it is reserved for Nate Baldwin. Last time I checked, I don't drive a Fiat. Please do NOT park in this spot again. Sincerely, NATE BALDWIN.

I smile in satisfaction as I place the note beneath the windshield wiper. That should teach them. The one thing I demanded when I came on board with Vincent's plan to start this hotel chain was a reserved parking spot. I know, it sounds ridiculous, but it's one of those status things I've always wanted. Now that I have it, I refuse to let some Fiat-driving asshole take it from me.

"Good morning, Josie," I say walking into my office.

"Good morning, Mr. Baldwin. Your nine o'clock is running late. Mr. Stafford's secretary called this morning and said he got a flat tire on the 294 this morning. Should I reschedule it? She said he would probably be about an hour late."

I glance at my watch. "No, it's okay if he's late. I have some paper-work I need to go over anyway, and Vincent mentioned something about a trip to Denver for that acquisition. I'll be in my office." I point toward the double doors as I make my way through them.

I shut the doors and walk over to my desk, seeing that my green smoothie is already there. Josie must be gunning for a raise going the extra mile like that. I pick it up, taking a long sip as I settle in to start my day.

"Vince?" I knock on his half-open door as I let myself in. He's chatting with his assistant as he waves me in.

"Hey, Nate, thanks for stopping by. I wanted to discuss the Denver acquisition with you really quick." I make my way toward his desk as I hear footsteps behind me. I turn around just in time to see Elise waltzing in with her perfectly styled curls bouncing in time with her steps. She blatantly ignores me, giving Vince and his assistant a sweet smile and a cheery 'good morning.'

She's wearing that god damn blue dress again, with bright red lips. It's navy blue and hits just above her knee. I don't know what kind of material you'd call it, but it's the type that clings to her skin, accentuating every curve. To most men, it would probably just be a dress, nothing provocative or over-sexualized, but it teases me just enough that I can feel myself start to harden and my mouth go dry. She crosses her long legs as she takes a seat and I can smell the sweet scent of vanilla waft up. I hurriedly sit down before I make a tent in my pants so big Boy Scouts could camp under it.

"So, I know you both saw the vague email I sent, but I needed to finalize a few things before I officially sent you both to Denver."

I glance over at Elise just as she glances at me. "Both?" I say with a raised eyebrow.

"Yes, both. Will that be a problem?" He steeples his fingers like he's a dad scolding us.

"Nope, not at all." I shake my head.

"Anyway, I have a previous engagement in Canada, but I need you both to go meet with the board there and finalize some financials and contract stuff. Very basic stuff you both can do in your sleep. It will only be for a few days."

We finish up the meeting, and I glance at my watch as I make my way toward the elevator. Mr. Stafford should be arriving at any minute. "You enjoy your smoothie this morning?" Elise asks as she sidles up next to me, looking me up and down. The doors open, and we both step inside.

"See something you like?" I ask, ignoring her question. I figure she's referring to the episode that occurred the other day in the lunchroom when she distracted me, causing the smoothie to explode all over me. I clench my hand at the thought. I'm still pissed at her for that one, but I wouldn't mind bending her over, pulling up that god damn dress, and anger banging the hell out of her right now.

"Hardly. I'd just hate for you to miss your morning smoothie. You know what they say: fruits and vegetables help keep us regular." I scrunch my face in confusion at her remarks as the elevator opens to our floor.

"What is that supposed to mean?" I look down the hall towards my office, seeing that Mr. Stafford has arrived and is talking with Josie. I give him a smile and wave as I turn to finish my conversation with Elise, who is halfway down the hall toward her office. Then it hits me...she's the one who put my smoothie on my desk.

I sprint down to catch her. "What the hell did you do, Elise?" I whisper-shout, trying not to cause a scene. My stomach rumbles and lets out an unnatural, animalistic sound.

"Good luck with that," she says with a syrupy fake grin before shutting the door in my face. I slam my fist against it as a sharp pain radiates up my arm, and I turn to make my back to my office for my meeting.

For the next hour, my stomach feels like it's on the verge of bottoming out and turning my ass into a very unpredictable volcano. Drops of sweat bead on my forehead as I try to listen to what Mr. Stafford is talking about. I nod and glance over the financials in front of me. He is the Senior Director at Bender & Wallace Wealth Management, a Certified Exit Planning Advisor and a Certified Merger & Acquisition Advisor with over 27 years of experience. The man knows his shit, but all I can't focus on is just trying not to shit my pants.

Finally, the meeting concludes, and I shut my door, locking myself in my private bathroom for the next hour. I'm done playing nice... Elise Taylor is about to meet her match. I walk back to my desk to find the napkin I had left on the Fiat earlier this morning. It has a response written in bright red lipstick.

Dear Mr. Baldwin, last time I checked...nobody gives a shit.

7

ELISE

"Things going better at work?" Tessa plops down on my bed as I pack up my things. I finally found a great apartment in the city that not only checks all my boxes but is a quick twenty-minute commute to work.

"A little. This month has flown by, and I think I just might have taught Nate a lesson, so he's been keeping his distance." Truthfully, I kind of hated that he had been avoiding me, for as much as he annoyed me to the point of homicide, I still got butterflies when I saw him walking down the hall. That man in a tailored suit could make an angel fall.

"Taught him a lesson?" Tessa props herself up on her elbows, so she can see me sitting on the floor.

"Uhhh, yeah. We kind of had this prank war going on, and let's just say I won."

"Oh god, what'd you do?" I can't help but burst into laughter as I tell her how I laced his smoothie with a laxative. At first, she's appalled, but soon she's rolling around in laughter with me. It feels like we're back in college again. I'm going to miss this.

"You're an evil genius, you know that? It's a good thing you're a lawyer or you'd probably be in prison yourself."

* * *

IT'S THURSDAY MORNING, and I'm rummaging through my desk drawers in search of the stylus for my iPad. I glance at the clock, "Shit, I'm late!" I finally find it in the bottom drawer, grabbing it, I run to the conference room for our weekly staff meeting. I scurry into the room and realize the only seat left at the large oval table is all the way in the front. I make my way to the front and place my items on the table while I take a seat.

I glance up and notice a few people staring at me with quizzical looks on their face but ignore it. Waking up my iPad, I notice a large, black smudge on the screen, *what the hell?* I glance at the front of my white blouse and see that it has transferred all over the front of it. I let out a sigh of frustration; no wonder everyone was looking at me. I grab a napkin from the pile on the table next to the donuts and try to rub it off my screen but it's thick and greasy, only making it worse.

"Pssst." I glance up to see Cheryl from accounting pointing to her upper lip and then to me. I look at her confused; I don't have time right now. I ignore her, but she repeats the gesture, so I pull open my iPad and flip the camera around. My face has large black streaks on it! The thick, greasy substance is now all over my iPad screen, my blouse, fingers, and a large spot above my eyebrow and upper lip.

I audibly gasp before gathering my things. Vincent looks over at me, stopping his speech and giving me a perplexed look as I hear the very distinct chuckle of Nate Baldwin.

I put my head down and dash out of the room and straight to the bathroom. I'm so angry and literally scream as I slam my things down on the counter. I quickly check under the stalls before locking the door and trying my hardest to scrub this shit off myself.

My face is red and angry from the furious scrubbing it took with a bathroom paper towel to get the substance off. My shirt is completely ruined; it's now wet and see-through with a massive grayish-black muddied stan all over the front of it. I gather my things and make my way back to my office.

I slam the door to my office and lean my back against it, letting out a large audible exhale. "I can't work like this." Tears prick my eyes and slam my fist against the back of my door. I'm angry. Angry that I let Nate get the best of me, and angry that I care so much. I would love to hate him, but the reality is...I want him. I can see he's the same fun-loving, charming guy I knew and fell in love with in college. More than anything, though—I would love to sit on his gorgeous face.

I toss my things on my desk and get to work on the contracts I need to go over. I have so much to get done before my trip to Denver. I try to focus, glancing at the clock several times over the next few hours until I can't take the tension any longer. My shirt is now dry, but the smudgy mess is a dull, dried stain that is scratchy to the touch. I smooth down the front of it anyway and straighten my skirt. I reach for the mirror in my desk drawer and double-check the makeup I reapplied after the redness and irritation from earlier had subsided. I slick on a fresh coat of gloss, add a touch of perfume, and fluff up my hair. "Moment of truth," I say as I walk out of my office and march towards Nate's.

"Mr. Baldwin, Miss Taylor is here to see you. Can I send her in?"

"Uhh, yes." I could hear the shock in Nate's voice, most likely since I actually waited outside of his office this time and spoke with his admin instead of busting in to take my revenge on him.

I smile sweetly at Josie as I make my way through the door. Nate is sitting at his desk with the palms of his hands lying flat against the wood. "To what do I owe the pleasure, Miss Taylor?" He still has the same cocky smirk he had from this morning when I ran out of the conference room. Remembering that makes my rage bubble up again and I'm tempted to say *fuck it* and launch myself across his desk to claw his fucking eyes out. Instead, I take in a deep yoga breathe and let it go.

"May I?" I ask, motioning to the chair to my left since he didn't offer me a seat.

"Please."

"So," I fold my hands in my lap and look him square in the eye. "I've been thinking, and I feel like this—situation between us," I motion with my finger, "has run its course. Don't get me wrong, I enjoy a good rival, and I certainly am not one to back down from a competition, but it's just getting a little out of hand. Don't you think?"

He's eyeing me skeptically. "Is this some kind of trap?"

"Nope. Just an old-fashioned truce. I'm not saying we need to be friends and braid each other's hair or anything, but maybe we could pump the brakes on the pranks? What do you say?" I give him my sweetest smile.

"I'm a little taken aback, Elise; I gotta be honest. After this morning, I fully expected you to come in here, guns blazing. Ready to rip my balls off and maybe throw a fire ant farm down my pants."

"So you admit that was your handiwork this morning?"

"Uh, no, I didn't say that, just that I figured you would assume it was me." He gives me a toothy grin before standing up. "Elise Taylor, I officially accept your truce," he says, thrusting his hand out towards me.

I reciprocate, standing and taking his hand with a pursed-lip smile. "Pleasure doing business with you, Mr. Baldwin." I spin on my heel and walk out of the office.

* * *

I GLANCE at the clock and realize it's almost seven already. I lean back in my chair and stretch my stiffened back while letting out an exaggerated yawn. I stand up and start gathering my things when a soft knock on my door startles me. I look up to see Nate leaning against the door frame.

"I'm surprised to see you here this late. Vince got you burning the midnight oil on something?" God, he looks like a walking wet dream standing there. His hair is disheveled like he's been running his hands through it. Like freshly fucked hair. I snap out of it, realizing I'm staring at him with my mouth hanging open.

"Something like that. What has you here so late?" I say, continuing to shut down my laptop, slipping it into my bag.

"I was just trying to get some things done before our trip to

Denver," he says, glancing nervously at his shoes. "Hey, so I actually am glad I caught you. I uh…I wanted to apologize."

That catches my attention. I stop what I'm doing and fold my arms across my chest, the signal for *keep going*.

"Yeah, I just thought a lot about things after you left this afternoon and honestly, I felt like a complete asshole. I was behind the shoe polish this morning."

"Ah, shoe polish," I said, my question about what the substance was answered.

"Yes. It was totally out of line and below the belt and every other analogy. Thanks for being the bigger man, er, woman in this situation and being willing to—"

Before he could finish, I was reaching for his tie, pulling him forward until he stumbled against me and his lips met mine. Confusion marred his beautiful face.

"Wha—Elise?" He places his hands on my shoulder and slightly pushes me away.

"Just shut up and kiss me," I say as I wrap my arms around his neck and deepen the kiss, thrusting my tongue into his mouth. His hesitation dissolves as his hands move from my shoulders down my arms and then to my waist. He grips my hips and walks me backward, pushing me until my back hits the wall roughly.

My desire consumes me. At the moment, I don't care. I don't care that we're coworkers. I don't care that he fucked me over ten years ago. I want him. Now. I can feel his cock growing harder and harder against my belly, and I reach down to palm him through his dress pants. He lets out an audible hiss as he lets his head fall back and his hips thrust harder against me.

"You fucking tease," he grits out as he lifts me, causing my legs to involuntarily wrap around his waist. He walks us towards my desk and sits me down as his lips move from mine down to my neck. His hands grip my thighs before sliding up, causing my skirt to lift and bunch around my waist. "This is already ruined," he says grabbing my blouse and pulling it apart, causing the buttons to pop off and skitter to the floor and across the surface of the desk.

I want him to stop talking, to take me fast and rough, but he stops his assault on my neck and leans back at my exposed torso. My breasts rise and fall with each breath, and I'm certain my nipples are so hard they could cut glass. He reaches out with both hands and cups them through my sheer bra before leaning down and sucking a nipple through the material.

I gasp, and my legs instinctively wrap around him tighter, pulling him closer to me. I can feel the rigid head of his manhood pressing against my clit, and I rock my hips in a forward motion against it. I try shrugging the shirt the rest of the way off of my body; he reaches up and helps me before ever so slowly pulling the straps of my bra down my arms. I want to see him, so I reach out and unbutton his shirt; thank god he isn't wearing an undershirt. Each muscle of his abs is straining against the tanned skin it's encased in. I stare at him, wanting to run my tongue over every inch of his chiseled body.

"What are you thinking?" he asks, never taking his eyes off my now bare tits.

"I don't want to be thinking at all. Just feeling." I reach out and unbuckle his belt before sliding the zipper down and reaching inside to wrap my hand around his rock-hard dick. He groans and squeezes his eyes shut as pinches one of my nipples. I stroke him up and down a few times as his hips begin to move in time with my strokes. He leans down again, this time biting my nipple and causing a shot of electricity to run straight to my clit. I squeeze him tighter, which causes his eyes to pop back open; this time they're hooded and heavy with lust. It's like I've awakened an animal.

He reaches down and rips my panties from my body with what sounds like a low growl before running his finger up and down my wet slit. "You're drenched, baby." I almost roll my eyes at the generic term of endearment.

"Please just shut up and fuck me," I say as I reach out to pull his dick out completely. He doesn't waste any time. He shoves my hand away and grips himself at the base, lining up the head with my entrance before slowly pressing against me.

I don't remember him being so big; granted, it's been a decade, but

I wince a little at the pain. He doesn't relent. Instead he takes a step forward, thrusting himself even further inside me. I look down and see his huge cock slowly sliding in and out of me, glistening with my own wetness, and it's exactly what I need. I feel myself relax and open up to him as I lean back on my elbows, propping myself up to watch his abs ripple with each movement of his hips.

His thrusts become harder, faster, and my tits sway and bounce with every move. His hips slap against my ass as he takes me deeper, both of us panting and moaning. I move my eyes up to his face and see he's staring at me, his eyes bouncing from mine to my lips to my breasts. I need to cum; the intensity is building, and I'm so close.

"Suck my nipples," I say breathlessly. "I ne—need to cum." I can barely get the words out as he obeys my command, leaning forward to lick and suck my nipples before biting down on one. I can't hold back any longer; I squeeze my legs against his hips as I reach down and touch my clit, an explosion of ecstasy rolling through my body. I don't even recognize the sounds coming from my lips as I moan and shout his name.

He's right behind me, thrusting erratically before suddenly pulling out, fisting his cock and then spilling himself all over my chest. He strokes himself until he's released every last drop, then wipes the head of his cock against my bare skin.

"What the fuck was that?" I ask. I can't hide my annoyance as he stuffs himself back in his pants and walks to pick up my ruined shirt.

"We didn't use protection, and this is already ruined." He shrugs. Before I can stop him, he's wiping the remnants of himself off my chest with my stained blouse.

"What the fuck!" I jump off the desk and grab the blouse from his hand. "Ruined or not, it's the only shirt I have, so how the hell am I supposed to walk out of the building now?" I can see he didn't think it through but doesn't seem bothered.

"Relax, you can wear my shirt. I have my gym bag in my office, and I'll just change into those clothes. I still need to work out anyway."

I grab the shirt from his outstretched hand and place it over my bare breasts. I'm suddenly very aware of my nakedness. I reach down and pick up my torn underwear. "And these?"

"Well, I have extra boxers in my bag too," he says with this stupid toothy grin. I roll my eyes and start to dress myself as he stands watching me.

"You can leave now," I say, turning away from him to clasp my bra before shrugging on the oversized shirt.

"Are we going to talk about this or…?" He trails off, not finishing his thought.

"No. It was just something we needed to get out of systems. Just a casual, no-strings-attached hookup. Something I've heard you're very well versed in."

He nods his head. "Lovely bedside manner. Ok then, have a good night, I guess." He turns to walk away.

"Oh, and Baldwin, don't worry about calling me this time."

8

NATE

I've done little this weekend but replay the scene from Friday night in Elise's office over and over in my head. Despite what she thinks, I've never had a hookup like that before. A woman who knows exactly what she wants and isn't afraid to go after it? Now that's hot as hell. The only problem is I want more. I want to see her in so many other positions, on all fours taking me deep and hard, on her knees in front of me with those delicious, juicy lips wrapped around my cock.

I groan and roll out of bed; I need to get my game face on. She and I have a flight to Denver today, and the last thing I need is a set of raging blue balls in that tight of quarters with no escape. Thankfully Vince is letting us take the company's private jet, so we don't need to deal with the hassle of other travelers.

This should make for an interesting trip. Elise made it seem like Friday night was a one-time thing, but I won't let that happen, not if I can help it. I'm going to get my fill of Elise Taylor before she kicks my ass to the curb again for another ten years.

* * *

"Here, I recommend you drink a few of these on the flight." I hand her a bottle of water as she takes her set.

"Thanks for the unsolicited hydration tip, Nate." She grabs it out of my hand before tossing it in the empty seat across from her.

"Do you ever take it out of bitch mode? I was just trying to offer some friendly advice seeing as how Denver is a mile above sea level and Vince told me you'd never been." I can see her roll her eyes as she ignores my comment and pulls her iPad out of her bag. I took a long, healthy glance at her ass when she boarded the flight; her dark wash skinny jeans hug her in all the right places. Now that I know exactly how that ,supple ass feels in my hand it makes a million times harder to focus.

"Are you going to be weird about things now?" she asks without looking up from the screen in front of her. I hadn't even realized I was staring at her, my eyes fixated on that small dip at the base of her throat. There's no question Elise is hot. I'm talking the kind of hot that guys will tear their arm off for just so they have something to give her. She's also beautiful and delicate. I continue to watch her slim, manicured hands dance across the keyboard on the screen as she absentmindedly chews on her bottom lip. A small tendril of hair has escaped her ponytail, and without thinking, I reach over and brush it off of her neck.

"What are you doing?" She swats my hand away as her shoulders bunch tensely up to her ears.

"Sorry, you just had a small piece of ha—never mind." I turn back to the water bottle in my hand and finish it in two large gulps. "Actually, why did you sleep with me if you hate me so much?"

Her mouth pops open, and she glances around the cabin as if anyone here will care or even heard me. "Jesus, Nate, just announce it to the world, why don't you."

"Oh, so now I'm your dirty little secret, huh? Okay, I see. Memo received." I try to sound cool and nonchalant, but I can't help it reflecting in my clipped, short statements. I glance over at her briefly, and it looks like her face softens a bit, but she just turns away and looks out the window as the captain makes his pre-takeoff announcements.

* * *

THE NEXT FEW days are going to be straight hell. Elise is dressed in a candy apple red dress that flows across her hips and hugs her breast. I try to stay focused on the meeting we're in, but my mind keeps wandering to thoughts of burying my face in her cleavage. The speaker drones on, so I take the opportunity to look at the shoes she's wearing: a pair of matching red strappy heels that wrap around her ankle.

Images of those dancing around my ears permeate my thoughts when I hear a slight cough and look to my right to see her staring daggers at me. Instead of averting my gaze, I let my eyes drop back down to her legs and lick my lips. Maybe I'm crazy, but I swear she squeezes her thighs together. I glance back up at her, and she's ignoring me, staring ahead as she slowly unclasps her ankles and seductively slides one leg over the other, allowing her dress to ride up a little. I can feel myself stiffen in my pants. *Christ, the smallest movement from her, and I'm losing my mind.*

I turn myself back towards the front of the room as I let my hand slip under the table and rest it softly on her knee. I feel her jerk a little at the intrusion and then sit up straighter. I let my hand linger for a moment before readjusting myself in my chair and allowing it to slide off her thigh. She squeezes her legs tighter, refusing to allow me entrance. I pinch her leg a little, causing a sharp inhale of breath before she relaxes, and I reach my hand under her dress even further until I glide across the small scrap of silk at the apex. I can hear her breathing now, and I can feel her growing damp. I press firmly against her clit as I rub it furiously, I'm sure she's on the edge because I can see her knuckles growing white as she grips the table and a small bit of space has formed between her lips. I look over at her eyelids that are hanging low and heavy. She's there; she's so close.

"I believe Elise Taylor, our in house counsel, has a few thoughts on that, Derek. Elise?" I pull my hand away as her eyes grow wide with horror, and her cheeks grow instantly red. A small sheen of sweat is on her forehead as she riffles through her papers, trying to gather herself. A huge grin spreads across my face as everyone turns their attention to her.

"I—I'm sorry, Derek, can you repeat what you were saying?"

Two hours later, she's pounding on the door of my hotel room, her eyes narrowed with anger. "Open up, Baldwin. I know you're in there, you asshole!"

I take my time opening the door, making sure I'm wearing nothing but the low-slung towel I wrapped around my hips after my shower. "How fu—" I don't let her finish. I pull her towards me and grab a handful of her curls, tipping her head back to take her mouth. She resists at first, pushing against my chest for a mere second before she's clawing at me, trying to get closer.

I spin her around, unzipping her dress and removing her bra and panties. "Leave the shoes on," I command before I shove her back on the bed. I remove my towel and grab my cock, stroking myself a few times as I look down at her gorgeous naked body on display. "Fuck it out of me, Elise. That's how you can take your frustration out on me." I don't have to tell her twice before she's pushing me back on the bed and climbing on top of me.

* * *

"Leave me alone," she mumbles into the pillows as I rip the sheets from her still-naked body. I give her ass a hearty smack.

"Get up; you promised me you'd go on a hike today."

"My head is killing me," she says as she reaches for the half-drunk water bottle on the nightstand.

I pull the curtains back as light floods the room, and she squints. "I'm not going to say I told you so, but that's exactly why I said to drink a lot on the flight. You have a little altitude sickness. Some fresh air will do you good." She groans and grunts, making her way around the room to gather her clothes from last night before slipping into her adjoining room. "Be ready in thirty. No need for all that makeup and hair and nails bullshit; it's just the mountains."

She flips me the bird before shutting the door to her room.

* * *

"Okay, looks like the trailhead is just up ahead. This trail is marked as 'easy.' I specifically picked one that had as little elevation gain as possible, but we still need to pace ourselves and make sure we don't burn out halfway through." She grabs the bottle from my hand as she pushes past me on the trail.

"I've done triathlons, Nate; I'm sure I can handle a little three-mile hike in the Rockies." I've never met such a bullheaded, hard-nosed woman in my life, but I let her set the pace. Besides, I can't deny the view of her ass bouncing in those tiny little short is more than motivating.

"Oh my god, I'm dying. I'm actually dying. I think my lungs are going to explode!" Elise grabs at her throat dramatically as she doubles over on the trail.

"So do I get an apology now or later?" I hand her the water and glance at my GPS watch. "The top is just over this ridge, so come on. The view will be worth it." We round the top and just as I predicted, the view clears and it's breathtaking.

I look over to see Elise scrambling over a large boulder, trying to get a better view. Her ass is up in the air, and her hands are down on the rock in front of her. I laugh as she struggles to find the next place to put her foot. "Laugh all you want, Baldwin; you wish you could get me in this position." I can't miss the opportunity, so I pull out my phone and snap a quick photo of her.

"Did you just take a picture of me?"

I double over in laughter as I look at the image on my screen. "You look like a wild animal!" I say between fits of laughter. Without hesitation, she skitters down the boulder, marches over to me, and grabs my phone—launching it off the mountain and down into the valley below.

9

ELISE

"I just—I don't get it, Tessa. He's either rocking my world and giving me mind-blowing, toe-curling, gut-punch orgasms, or he's being an arrogant ass-bag that I want to punch in the face." I flick my hair over the edge of my lawn chair, enjoying the last of the Chicago sun before the brisk temperatures of autumn roll in.

I glance over at her, noticing she isn't responding. "What? What's with the judgy face? Just say it, Tessa." I pull my glasses off my face and swing my legs around to face her.

"I didn't say anything; you are just overreacting because you already know the answer." She takes a long sip of her drink, never breaking her intense eye contact with me.

"No, no. NO! There are no feelings here. We both knew that this was an itch we needed to scratch and he's completely not the dating type. He's like the dirty sexy secret type that you have hot sweaty car sex with in the parking garage at your office after work...and before work...and sometimes at lunch."

"Christ, you guys are like rabbits! You're telling me that through all of this ridiculous and dirty teenage humping, you don't feel even a flicker of something?"

I feel a little pit in my stomach, the bad kind of pit. The pit that is small and nagging and screaming all at the same time for you to run for your life. "No." I lie.

"Well, I bet he does then. You are way too old to still think that friends with benefits is a thing that doesn't end in heartache. If I were you, I'd either get out now or see if it could turn into something."

I glance away, picking up my wine and downing the rest of it. I know she's probably right. Maybe I should have a talk with Nate on Monday, break things off before they get completely out of hand.

"Now can we pleeeease stop talking about you and Nate so that I can tell you about this hot dancer I met the other night?"

"Ohhh, do tell! Like a stripper?" I squeal like I'm still a silly seventeen-year-old.

"What? No, like a real dancer. She competes in ballroom stuff, and she teaches at a studio in Lincoln Park, which is where I met her."

"You're taking dancing lessons? You, who chipped a tooth at prom trying to do the worm?"

"Hey, we are going to leave that detail off the table, ok? I met her at a bar through some mutual friends, and we hit it off, so I signed up for dance lessons. What's sexier than private salsa lessons? Give me a month, and I'll be ripping up the floor at your and Nate's wedding."

* * *

MONDAY MORNINGS ARE ALREADY UNWELCOME, but today especially, the dread was turned up to eleven. I thought long and hard over the weekend about what Tessa had said, and I made my decision: I need to end things with Nate. While I like to fully ignore the growing feelings that I know I have for him, I am just about positive he doesn't feel the same way. I'm like one of the guys to him, someone he can high five when he sees a hot girl with huge boobs and then can booty call over the weekend.

We haven't even been on an actual date; all of our alone time has consisted of hushed hookups in the work stairwell or staying late so he can bend me over his desk. We haven't even hooked up outside of the office building besides our little getaway to Colorado. We are work friends who hook up, nothing more.

I sent him a message earlier to see if he could swing by my office and he said he'd make some time this afternoon, so I set about chewing through some emails and following up on a few phone calls. I am just about to grab a second cup of coffee when my phone chirps with a text message from my mom.

Hey, Elise, it's Mom. Can you please call home?

My drops to my stomach. Ever since my dad's stage-three cancer diagnosis nine months ago, I've been on edge when I receive a text like that. I take a deep breath and hit the dial button.

"Hey, Mom, how's it going?"

"Just can't get enough, can you, Taylor?" Nate says, barging into my office. My back is turned toward him, and I'm staring out the window as the reality of what my mom just told me is sinking in. I can't help the tears that fall from my eyes and run down my cheeks.

"We're going to have to make this quick; I have a call in thirty." He takes his suit coat off and tosses it onto one of the chairs as he walks up behind me and unzips my skirt.

"Not right now," I say pulling the zipper back up and stepping away from him. I hastily wipe the tears away and try not to let him see my face.

"Geez, you get your period between when you texted me this morning and now?"

"Nate, please. You can harass me all you want tomorrow but I ju—" I can't hold back the sob that escapes my lips.

"Whoa, whoa, Elise, what's going on?" I can see the genuine concern on his face as he steps toward me and places a hand on each shoulder. "I'm sorry, I was just giving you a hard time. Is everything ok?"

All I can do is shake my head no as I wipe the snotty, teary mess from my face. He reaches over on my desk and grabs me some tissues. "What's going on?"

"It's my dad." I take in a long, shaky breath trying to get my crying under control. Nate pulls me in for a hug and runs his hand over my back softly.

"Shhh, you don't need to explain right now. It's okay just to let it out." I don't understand what's happening, but I comply, letting go of the emotions that pour out of me in a flood. My shoulders shake as I bury my face in the crook of his neck.

I don't know how long I stand there, but it feels like an eternity as he continues to rub my back and every so often kisses my hair. Finally, I pull myself away from him. His shirt is wet with my tears and smeared with makeup. "I'm sorry," I say, brushing at the wet stain with my overused and crumpled tissues.

"Don't apologize," he says softly as he takes my face in his hands and plants a soft kiss on my lips. He grabs my hand and leads me over to the small loveseat in my office. "Do you want to talk about it?"

I stare at my hands, fiddling with the tissue. "Nine months ago, my dad was diagnosed with stage-three brain cancer. They found a small mass and removed it, but the doctor said there's always a chance it could come back. After two rounds of chemo and radiation, he was cancer-free. Back to his old self, back to work and feeling great. My mom called me this morning..." I stop to compose myself, still in shock at the news. I glance up at the ceiling trying to will myself not to cry again.

"She said that my dad hasn't been feeling very well for the last few weeks and he hid it from her. She noticed that he was saying weird words in place of the right ones, and he couldn't remember where he left things. She finally managed to convince him to go back to the oncologist, and they got his MRI results back yesterday. He has two more masses on his brain, one on his lungs, and two on his liver."

Nate reaches over and wraps an arm around me as I start to sob again. "They only gave him a few months...I don't know what I'm going to do, Nate."

"I'm so sorry, Elise. I—I don't know what to say."

I compose myself and stand, walking over to my desk to grab some water. "Thanks, Nate. I know things are carefree with us and not exactly deep, so I appreciate it, really. I think I need to tell Vince that I'll be gone for a few days. I need to go home and be with my family."

He stands from the couch and nods as he heads toward the door. "If you need anything, please don't hesitate to reach out. I mean it."

I stand, staring at the floor for a moment after he leaves. I can feel my body swaying. I step back and sit on the edge of my desk for a moment before sending a message to Vincent and heading to my apartment.

* * *

IT'S ALMOST nine when I sit down on my couch. I managed to get work stuff wrapped up and pack for my trip in the morning. I could have left tonight, but I'm in no state to be behind the wheel of a car for five-plus hours. I flip through some old photos on my phone that I took with my dad a few years ago when a soft knock on my apartment door startles me. I walk over and open it slowly to see a sullen Nate on the other side. A bottle of wine in one hand and a small overnight bag and flowers in the other.

"What are you doing here?" I ask, slightly hiding behind my door, realizing I'm in a very oversized and holy t-shirt with no pants.

"I couldn't let you be alone tonight, Elise. Can I come in?"

I step aside and motion for him to come in. He places the bag on the floor and hands me the flowers. "Can we talk?" he asks.

"Yeah, let me put these in some water, and I could really use that wine if you don't mind," I say reaching, out and taking it from him. I put the flowers in a vase and pour us both a glass of wine before retreating to the couch.

"Listen," he says while reaching out to grab my hand. "I want to be here for you. I want to go with you to see your family. I know it's an intrusion, but I don't feel like you should be driving that far alone."

"Okay." I reach over and grab my glass from the table.

"Really? No fight?" he says, a small smile forming at one corner of his mouth. "Never thought I'd see the day." He pulls me toward his chest, and I fall back against him. He stretches his long legs out on the couch, and my back is against his chest as he gently rubs small circles in my neck.

"Tell me about him," he says as I open my phone and flip back through the photos.

10

NATE

THREE MONTHS LATER...

I t's been three months since Elise got the news about her dad and things took a turn for the worse drastically and rapidly after our visit. You wouldn't even know the man was sick by looking at him, which is part of what made it all so hard on her. I was selfishly a little worried that it would be uncomfortable to be there, but her family was so welcomingly and loving.

Her parents didn't put any pressure on me to define what we were, another selfish fear I had. What would I tell her dying father? Things just fell into place. We went out to dinners and took long walks around the lake that backed up to their yard. I played fetch with the family dog while Elise made a fresh peach pie with her mother and her father just sat on a bench near the water and watched us play.

There was a sadness in the air, but it didn't stop the family from laughing and enjoying the moments that they had left to share.

After Elise and I returned home, we just sort of fell into a pattern. I would pop into her office to share lunch, and she'd tell me how her dad was doing. We still had intimate moments here and there, mostly when Elise was feeling sad and vulnerable. I was happy to provide her with that release, that escape from the knowledge that there was nothing she could for her family.

I put my feelings on hold. I wanted to support her in any way that I could. She spent most weekends back home, so we only saw one another at the office and on the nights when she'd text me and ask me to come over. Those nights were either spent in her bed, our bodies expressing our feelings, or on her couch where I would hold her while she cried.

She had her ups and downs; some days were better than others, but this week was the worst. Elise had left early on Tuesday and sent me a message late Tuesday night that she had driven to her parents. By Wednesday morning, I was in my car, on my way to be with her. I didn't even think twice; I threw some clothes in a bag, jumped in my car, and sent her a quick text.

I'm on my way.

"You want some company?" I poke my head around her bedroom door and see her sitting on her bed. Her long hair is cascading down her back as she stares at the window.

A small smile spreads across her beautiful lips as she pats the bed next to her. I shut the door and make my way to take a seat.

Her dad passed away Wednesday night; it was peaceful. As peaceful as can be expected. Elise and her mother already made most of the funeral arrangements, but the last few days were spent finalizing things, and of course, attending the actual funeral and graveside services. It had been small but it felt like the entire town was there. Her parents were loved and respected in the community.

"How are you doing?" I ask, rubbing her back.

"Numb…but also at peace. I hated seeing my dad the way he was the last few months, and I know he hated it as well. My dad was always so strong and independent, one of those guys that knew how to fix everything and make anything with some wood and a few nails." A small giggle escapes her lips as if she's remembering a specific memory.

She sighs softly and leans her head on my shoulder. "In case I haven't said it enough, thanks for being here for through all of this. I know things have just been weird lately, we kind of did a complete one-eighty with our relationship...friendship? I don't know what to call it."

I wrap one arm around her shoulder and squeeze her. "Hey, that's what friends are for. I do have a serious question for you, though?" She cocks an eyebrow at me. "Can I please look through that yearbook I see on your shelf over there?" Before she can stop me, I bound off the bed and grab it. She tries unsuccessfully to grab it from me, but I find her portrait from junior year. I stare at it; she looks so young.

"I can see a resemblance, but man, this hardly even looks like you. What were you like in school?"

She flops back against her pillows, "You really wanna know?"

"Mmhmm," I say as I flip through the pages.

"Well, I was a bit of a loner. I was small and quiet, didn't say much to anyone. In fact, I bet if you went back and asked most of my classmates, they couldn't tell you who Elise Taylor was. If they do remember me, they'd probably say, 'Oh, that weird girl that hung out with teachers?'"

"What? You hung out with teachers?"

"I had like two friends, and one of them moved away after freshman year. The other friend was this super shy, awkward kid named Thomas Fillmore who had his own set of nerd friends that he often ditched me for."

I close the book and lean over on my side, propping myself up on my elbow to listen to her story.

"I actually skipped eighth grade, and I was already small for my age, so imagine being small and awkward as hell in seventh grade and then going into high school. My teachers tried to get me to skip two grades, but my parents said no. They thought it would make me too socially uncomfortable, and they were right. So anyway, there I was, looking like I still belonged in sixth grade, and I'm rubbing elbows with these high school girls that already have full C-cup boobs and hips. I felt like a corn dog among filet mignon."

I bust out laughing at her analogy, and she follows suit; it's so good to see her laughing again.

"All that to say the only person who talked to me and saw potential in me was Miss Sanders. She was a retired attorney who took up teaching because she loved kids and didn't have any of her own. She was my civics and government teacher, and she's the reason I became a lawyer. She used to tell me I had the mind for it, and she helped me find my voice."

She stares up at the ceiling, running a few fingers mindlessly through her hair. "And whatever happened to Miss Sanders?"

"She died about six years ago. I always kept in touch with her; she actually flew out to my graduations from Dartmouth and George-town. I went to her funeral and spoke at it. I was shocked to see how many students came back for it; she touched so many lives."

She continues telling me stories about her life growing up, and I'm amazed at the woman before me. She so strong and driven and has such love and passion for the people in her life. I can't help but hope I'm one of them. I watch her eyes crinkle as she laughs hysterically, telling me another story, and I feel like I've been punched in the stomach. I'm in love with this woman. Head-over-heels, knock-you-on-your-ass, once-in-a-lifetime kind of love.

That night, we made love in her childhood bedroom. Instead of feeling naughty and taboo, it felt amazing, like we were connecting on a new level. I was seeing her in a new light, a way I'd never looked at anyone, and I felt like she was doing the same.

I roll to my side and watch her sleep, small puffs of air escaping her lips with each exhale. I lean in and press a soft kiss to her forehead and take a moment to savor this memory. "I love you, Elise Taylor," I whisper against her forehead. I know now isn't the time to talk about our future or where things are going, and I'm okay with that, but I plan to soon.

The next morning, I head back home, giving Elise a few days to be with her mom alone. Just as I'm about to leave, her mom pulls me to the side. "Nate, I wanted to thank you for coming. Not just for all of us, but for Elise. She's…she's an independent child, but she needs love too, and I'm so thankful she has you." She pulls me in for a tight hug and then walks away. Guess I'm not the only one who can see things are changing.

11

ELISE

"So what exactly are we shopping for again?" Tessa asks as she riffles through a rack of clothes.

"My office Christmas party is on Saturday, and I need a dress that says *eat your heart out Nate Baldwin.*"

"What? I thought things were going well between you two? What happened now?"

"They are, they're good...they're stagnant. Honestly, I don't know where we stand. Ever since my dad's funeral a few months ago, he's been a little off. We still hang out and hookup, but it's like he's handling me with kid gloves. He's been way too nice, and it's starting to freak me out. It seemed like things were heating up and going in a really good direction, then he hit the brakes and jumped out of the damn car."

Tessa laughs, "God, girl, you need to pick a lane with this poor man. Odds are you guys just need to have that adult conversation we all dread: where is this going? What are we? Ya know, all that shit that ends up being the death of relationships. Does anyone at work know about you guys?"

"No, I don't think so. I'm not sure if we are actively hiding it but we just naturally haven't been openly affectionate in the office."

"I don't envy you; it's never fun sorting out the dynamics of a relationship. The are we, aren't we game."

"Ugh, I know. Love is so overrated. Disney needs to make a movie about that concept." I let my shoulders hang heavy.

"Love? Did you just say LOVE?" Tessa's eyebrows are raised as she practically shouts the last word.

"I just mean like in general. I didn't say I was in love. The general concept—you know what? Whatever. How are things going with you and Genevieve the dancer?"

"Why do you always have to say her name like that? She's not pretentious. They're going well; we are taking it very slow, and we're both happy about it."

I drag her to about seven more stores until I find the perfect dress: a long cream dress that's covered in beads and rhinestones with a very low back and a boat neck. As soon as I try it on Tessa actually gasps. I spin around in the floor-length mirror of the store. "You look like you're straight out of The Great Gatsby."

The dress highlights my curves and I can just imagine the lights of the ballroom bouncing off of it. Our party is in the grand ballroom of the flagship hotel location. "This dress will have him eating out of my hand for sure."

* * *

I step out of the Uber and make my way through the entrance of the hotel. They went all out for our party; there's a red carpet and a photo area. The men are all dressed in designer tuxes and the women in gorgeous gowns. There are white-gloved waiters walking around with champagne flutes and trays of delicious-looking hors d'oeuvres.

I glance around the large ballroom looking for Nate. We hadn't discussed coming together tonight; in fact, we hadn't talked about the part at all. I assumed as one of the executives, it's mandatory he shows up, but I can't know for sure.

I grab a glass of champagne and try to snag a bacon-wrapped

shrimp, snaking my way through the crowd. I spot Vincent, who waves me over with a tall model-looking blonde on his arm.

"Wow, you look fantastic!" she compliments my dress; her breathy, high pitched voice suits her perfectly.

"Thank you, you do as well. Hi, I'm Elise." I introduce myself, noticing Vincent hasn't made the effort.

"I'm Chloe. Nice to meet you." I make small talk with her and Vincent, but I'm not actually listening. Instead I continue to scan the room for Nate, offering up a head nod and short phrases now and then to sound interested.

I'm just finishing up my second glass of champagne when I see Nate walk in. He looks like a god damn Disney prince; I swear there's a ring of light around him as he smiles and waves to a few people in the room. He's wearing a black tux with a perfectly tied bowtie; he flashes that perfect smile to someone that approaches him and runs his hand through his gorgeously tousled hair. I smile as I set my empty glass on the tray of a passing waiter and start to make way over to him but stop dead in my tracks. Who the FUCK is that?

The crowd of people move as a waif-like model of a woman comes into view. She's tossing her head back and laughing, bouncy blonde curls moving in what looks like slow motion. Her eyes are bright and sparkling and her perfect pout a cherry red.

Not wanting to embarrass myself, I quickly turn on my heels and make my way through the crowd to a quieter part of the party. I spy a few people I've become friendly with from accounting and make my way over to them. Once again, I smile and nod at their conversation, but I'm not really listening. I watch Nate and the mystery woman glide around the ballroom, laughing and bull-shiting with everyone. I down a third glass of champagne and sulk at the pit that has formed in my stomach.

Sure, Nate and I hadn't had 'the talk' about our relationship yet, we hadn't even discussed exclusivity, but I figured he had enough respect for me to tell me when it was over instead of showing up to the party with his new conquest. The more I think about it, the more livid I become. I can feel my blood boiling and the champagne starting to give me the courage to approach him.

I see him break off from his date and make his way down the hallway towards the restrooms. Now is my chance. I practically toss my empty glass at a passing waiter and make my way down the hallway, lying in wait for Nate to emerge from the bathroom so I can attack. I pace a little, talking myself up and going over what I'm going to say to him.

I turn just as he's coming out of the restroom, a huge grin on his face as he sees me. "There you are, beautiful. Wow, you look fantastic!" he says, holding his arms out to me as if he's about to pull me in for an embrace.

"Excuse me?" I say with enough attitude to put a teenage girl to shame. I can see the confusion on his face as his hands drop to his sides.

"Who the fuck do you think you are?" I don't even try to hold back the volume of my voice as I jab a finger in his direction. "Showing up here with your next flavor of the month like I don't even matter!"

"Whoa, whoa, Elise, let me—" He tries interrupting me with an excuse, but I don't stop.

"No! You don't get to stomp all over me and make me feel like shit and try to feed me some bullshit line. I'm not letting you do that to me again!" I can feel tears start to sting my eyes as flashbacks to my college disappointment come flooding back to me. "How? I don't understand?"

"Well, if you'd let me get a word in, I can explain."

"Oh, don't you fu—" I roll my eyes and prepare to launch into my second diatribe when he raises his voice.

"Elise! Jesus, woman, don't you ever give it a rest? My god, you fly off the handle like you're unhinged instead of letting me explain." I stand back in shock; he's never yelled at me before.

"She's my sister. It's Shelly. I've told you about her."

"Hello?" I hear a woman's voice behind me, and I turn to see Shelly standing behind me. She waves nervously as she approaches. "I'm so sorry for the confusion, Elise; I really am his sister. This whole thing is my fault. He told me about the party, and I was in town for barely two days so I asked if I could come with him. It was my only chance to get to spend any real time with him. I was really excited to meet you."

She's sweet and genuine, and I feel like a complete asshole. I smile as I reach out a hand, wiping away the stray tear that has fallen down my cheek with my free hand. "Nice to meet you, Shelly." I turn back to face a very unamused Nate.

"I'm sorry I—" I start to speak but he holds up his hands.

"I need a few minutes; I'm going to get some air," he says before walking down the hall and pushing open a door.

I let out a sigh and look up toward the ceiling. "I really fucked up this time."

"Oh, don't worry about him," she says, coming up beside me to rub my shoulders. "Listen, he's an idiot for not telling you beforehand that he'd be showing up with a random woman, but I'm also sorry for taking this night away from you two. He told me he wanted to ask you tonight, as his girlfriend, and I've been dying to meet the woman who made my brother fall crazy in love."

My hand goes instinctively to my chest as I gasp, "Did you say—love? He loves me?" She covers her mouth before letting out a small laugh.

"Oh my god, have you guys not said that yet? I'm so sorry, I didn't know. Honestly, with the way he goes on and on about you, I was shocked you weren't living together when I arrived." I can't breathe. I feel like the room is spinning, and my heart is about to explode.

I don't even respond to Shelly. I just turn and run down the hall toward Nate. I throw the door open to see him standing on the edge of the sidewalk looking up at the stars.

"I'm in love with you," I say. He turns around slowly, his hands in his pocket.

"What?"

"You heard me."

"Say it again." A small smile breaks his stoic façade.

"I love you, Nate Baldwin. You're arrogant and condescending and infuriating—" He cuts me off when his lips land on mine, his hand darting to the back of my neck. I pull away a little as his wraps his other arm around my back.

"You're also kind and supportive and loving and wonderful, and you make me so happy." I try to choke back the tears as he pulls me to him again, his soft lips caressing my own.

He breaks the kiss and places a hand on either side of neck. "Elise, I have loved you from the moment you told me off in that elevator the first week you worked here. You try my patience like no other woman, but my god, you're so worth it."

I link my arms together around his neck as we kiss, the world and everything else melting around us.

EPILOGUE

ELISE-ONE YEAR LATER...

"I can't believe it's been over a year that you've been with Nate. You guys moving in together soon or what?" Tessa asks, taking a huge bite of the pizza we ordered.

"Who knows. I swear he moves at a snail's pace. We've talked about a future together, and he always says stuff like *when we have kids* or *when we're old,* but he still hasn't even hinted about ring shopping or maybe moving in together." I get up to grab another slice.

"A snail's pace? Elise, it hasn't even been two years, so calm down. Granted, I've never dated a guy, but in general, I think they are less apt than women to be jumping into engagement talk. It's like a repellent for them."

"I'm in no rush to get married; I'd just like to have a ring on my finger, ya know?"

"Okay, you say that, but I guaran-damn-tee you once you have that ring on, you'll be a bridezilla, demanding to set a date and picking out flowers and whatever. It's 2019, babe; who cares about tradition? Ask him already if you're that anxious about it."

"Ask him? As in propose?" I'm a little shocked at the suggestion.

"Yeah, why not? One of my friends at work just did. She got down on one knee and everything." I let Tessa's words roll around in my brain for a minute.

"Yeah, that's a good idea! I mean, why not? You're right; it's 2019, and we are strong, independent women who can do whatever the hell we want."

"Okay, calm down, Miss Suffragette; we still have a long way until we reach that status in this world."

* * *

I CHEW NERVOUSLY on my pen cap as I reread the contract on my desk for the third time. It's been a few days, and Tessa's suggestion is still rolling around in my head. I tried prodding Nate this weekend, asking him questions about honeymoons or where his dream wedding would take place, but I couldn't seem to get more than a few words out of him on the subject. I'm not one to sit around, so why not take things into my own hands?

I know without a doubt that Nate is the man I want to marry and spend the rest of my life with. I always smile when I think about our kids running around the backyard with him. Him teaching them soccer and building a treehouse.

After work, I slip into my workout clothes and throw on my running shoes, opting to hit the trail on Lake Shore Drive to clear my head. I don't even pay attention to the weather as large, dark storm clouds start to roll in. I continue pounding the pavement, one foot in front of the other as large, heavy raindrops start to pelt me.

I don't even think; I just run, letting my legs take me wherever, and soon I'm standing out front of Nate's apartment, soaking wet. I hit the buzzer on his building, and he lets me up. I'm still amped from the run; I try to calm my breathing in the elevator.

"Hey, babe, I wasn't expecting you tonight. I thought you said you had plans?" he says, placing a quick kiss on my lips. I remove my shoes in silence as he shuts the door behind me. "You're soaking wet; why in the world would you run in the rain?"

He walks to his room and comes back a minute later with a towel and some fresh clothes. "Here, put on some of my sweats and a t-shirt." I quickly change, tossing my wet clothes on the floor next to my shoes, and walk nervously behind him. In all of my thoughts about asking him to marry me, I never actually formulated what I was going to say.

Before I can back out, I drop to one knee. "Nate, wait."

"Hmm?" He turns around, and his eyes drop to where I'm at on the floor. "What the hell?"

"Nate Baldwin, I love you more than life itself. I never thought I would meet someone who ma—"

"No, no, get up Elise," he says, reaching down to pull me up by my elbows. "You're not going to do this."

"Why not? I want to marry you, Nate."

"And I want to marry you, Elise."

"Then why haven't you asked?" I wring my hands. I feel like a child being scolded, and I don't know why. He isn't angry, and he just told me he wants to marry me. I know I'm being childish, but tears start to form and tumble down my cheeks.

"Oh, sweetheart," he says with a laugh and pulls me in for a hug. "Dammit, woman, you can never just leave well enough alone and let things happen, can you?" He pulls me back and places his finger under my chin, tilting it upward till my gaze meets his. "You know how hard it is to get you to think I'm not constantly thinking about convincing you to marry me?"

I smile in relief, realizing that's why he's been avoiding any talk of marriage or moving in together. "I'm sorry. I just—I get myself worked up. I don't want to lose you again, Nate."

"Stay right here." He disappears for a minute before remerging with something in his hand.

"Elise, you will never lose me again. I can promise you that, right here, right now. Nothing in this world will tear me from you. I certainly didn't plan on doing this tonight but who cares." He opens his hand to reveal a small black box. "Honestly, I've been struggling like crazy to figure out how to ask you to marry me. You're a hard woman to hide stuff from." We both giggle as he opens the box to reveal a beautiful round diamond surrounded by a halo of smaller diamonds in a platinum band. I gasp as the light catches it.

Nate falls to one knee and takes the ring as he reaches for my hand. "Elise, there's nobody else like you in the world. You are not only my lover, but you're my best friend. Will you please also be my wife and the mother of my children?" All I can do is nod my head as tears stream down my face, and he slips the ring on my finger.

I pull his hand, and he stands, taking me in his arms. I giggle to myself a little as I remember the words Tessa told me that day she found me crying over him in my bed over ten years ago. *"You certainly won't remember Nate fucking Baldwin. I can promise you that."*

***

If you loved *Hate That I Love You*, don't miss out on *Business & Pleasure!*

Rich. Arrogant. So drop dead sexy you're ready to sell your kidney just to touch him.
Did I mention he's technically my new boss?

You know the type…
Every man wants to be him and every woman wants him.
Mr. Never-Goes-Home-With-The-Same-Woman- Twice guy.

I hate him but also…

GRAB BUSINESS & PLEASURE HERE!

BUSINESS & PLEASURE
SNEAK PEEK

Rich. Arrogant. So drop dead sexy you're ready to sell your kidney just to touch him.
Did I mention he's technically my new boss?

You know the type…

Every man wants to be him and every woman wants him.

Mr. Never-Goes-Home-With-The-Same-Woman- Twice guy.

I hate him but also...

Why can't I stop myself from seeing him on top of me every time I close my eyes?

Yeah…I'm screwed.

All I have to do is follow the rules.
1. Don't sleep with the sexy, arrogant prick.

2. Don't drool every time you look at his perfectly chiseled face and rock-hard body.

3. But mostly…don't let him know you want him just as bad.

Then again…rules are meant to be broken.

Can a no-strings-attached fling blossom into actual, head-over-heels love or will I ruin my career when I finally slap that smug grin off his panty-melting face?

GRAB BUSINESS & PLEASURE HERE!

CHAPTER 1

ALLISON

L ife has a funny way of not turning out the way you thought it would. Sometimes it's irony, other times it's a full-blown quarter-life crisis staring you in the face at twenty-five years old...in an airport bathroom.

It's crazy how one minute, you have your entire life planned out, and in a few short hours and a few impulsive, if not reckless, decisions later, your life has jumped the tracks and is now aimlessly barreling ahead at full speed.

I splash cold water on my face and take in a few deep breaths, hoping it will calm the symphony of butterflies in my stomach. My knuckles have gone white as I grip the edge of the sink, willing myself to stay calm and pull it together. I hardly notice the endless stream of fellow travelers coming in and out.

Once I'm calm enough, I reach into my purse and pull out a few makeup items to freshen myself up. What's that stupid quote about giving a woman the right lipstick and she can conquer the world? Yeah, okay, show me that color, please. The woman who penned that never had a quarter-life crisis in a public restroom.

After a little self-care and a mental pep talk, I feel good enough to emerge from my hideout, if only to make a beeline for the nearest bar. I feel a buzzing in my pocket as I exit the restroom and pull out my phone to check my messages.

"Uggghhh, goddammit!" I groan petulantly as I read the 'your flight is now delayed' text from my airline. I even throw in a foot stomp for emphasis as I roll my eyes and grab my bag, heading off in search of that bar.

Locating a decent-looking watering hole, I pull up my bag to a barstool and dramatically flop onto the seat. The bartender gives me a nod as if to say he sees me and will be over in a moment. I don't even need to look at the menu to know what I want.

I wasn't a big drinker in college, despite a stressful double major and a demanding internship. I enjoy a nice glass of wine now and then, but when I need to calm my nerves or feel a buzz, I always go for a dirty vodka martini with extra olives. I rattle off my order to the bartender when he finally saunters over, barely giving him the chance to get out his pleasantries.

The bar is dimly lit, even for an airport. It's located in a more obscure part of the terminal and seems to be the bar people go to when they have a long layover or are stuck with a shitty delay like myself. I barely have the first sip of my very overpriced martini when I feel the familiar presence of a once-popular frat boy lingering near me. Why do they all feel the need to douse themselves in enough mediocre cologne to offend anyone within a fifty-yard radius?

I set my drink back down when he leans himself against the bar, half-pressing himself against my arm as if personal space is a thing of the past.

"Looks like you could use another," he says as he sloppily points to my very full martini glass.

"I haven't even had a full drink of this one yet but thank you." I smile politely but turn away quickly so as not to encourage him.

This isn't my first rodeo; I am very aware of the effect I have on men. I was blessed by the genetic gods with piercing blue eyes and naturally thick blonde hair. I'm not Barbie height, merely five-six, but

I don't have to do much to keep my hourglass figure and perky C-cups. I can't complain, and I certainly don't take it for granted, but it pretty much attracts douchebags like it's their job. Sometimes I feel bad for them that they can't seem to resist a full-breasted blonde woman. Very predictable, and very pathetic.

My friends had given me the nickname Barbie since I was about thirteen years old. At the time, I had outgrown pretty much everyone in my grade and was the only middle schooler that stood head and shoulders above everyone else and had a full chest. Unfortunately, I stopped growing that same year. When I was younger, I was mortified by the attention my body got me; it was awkward as hell to be the only fifth grader wearing a sport's bra at recess to play kickball.

"So where you headed to? You live here in Dallas? I'd love to take you out sometime if you do. Or, hey, even if you don't, I'd fly to take you out!" He gestures wildly as he speaks, almost too confident that his offer to take me out will surely melt my panties and leave me begging him for happily ever after.

"No, no, I'm not local, and you haven't even asked my name or introduced yourself, but you want to take me out?" He quickly jumps in and cuts me off, thrusting his hand out to grasp mine.

"Trevor—"

I hold up my hand to stop him as I interject, "Don't bother. I won't remember it, and I won't be accepting the offer to hang out. I have had one helluva day, so if you don't mind, I'm going to drink this overpriced and watered-down martini in relative peace, ok?" I smile to soften the blow, but it doesn't seem to help.

He rolls his eyes and backs away with his hands in the air as if to say he surrenders. Something tells me he's probably been in trouble for his behavior in the past.

"You know, you blonde bitches are all the same. Your loss, sweetheart," he slurs.

I lift my martini glass to him with a huge grin as I turn back around to face the bar and drown my sorrows.

Relieved to no longer be gagging on the syrupy-sweetness of his cologne, I drum my fingers on the bar, unsure of what to do with myself or my time.

Normally, I would be elbows deep in a design, but since I had unceremoniously walked in on my ex banging someone else, I wasn't exactly in the headspace.

"That was a pretty brutal rejection; you seem well practiced at it though."

I haven't even noticed the man sitting to my left. There is an empty stool between us, but he clearly overhead my conversation with cologne boy.

I turn my head to give him a snarky remark, but my words catch in my throat and I quickly down two large gulps of my martini. The liquor burns my throat, but it allows me the few extra seconds I need to gather my thoughts.

This guy looks like he walked out of a catalog called *Sexiest Men Alive*. I know that's a stupid way to describe someone but imagine all those guys that are in luxury car commercials and Ralph Lauren ads. The ones that somehow look like they work on Wall Street, are a secret agent, and could also be the leader of the free world while saving babies in their spare time…that's this guy. It looks like the Greek gods hand-carved this guy to be their fucking mascot.

He cradles a tumbler of amber liquid as he shoots me a coy smile, waiting for my response. His hair looks like waves of dark chocolate with a dusting of gray at the temples, and his eyes are the most vibrant green I have ever seen. The way his tailored suit hugs his body, I can imagine he keeps himself in amazing shape.

Realizing I'm staring uncomfortably long at this stranger, I smile and shrug my shoulders at him, clearly still at a loss for forming coherent thoughts like a functioning adult.

"Cheers to a shitty day. I heard you tell Trevor over there that you had a helluva day and I can commiserate with you there."

"Who?" I can feel my face wrinkle in confusion.

"The lovely gentleman that just approached you," he says, gesturing with a nod towards the table of rowdy frat guys.

"Oh! Sorry, I guess I didn't even catch his name." I shrug my shoulders again as if this is the only form of primitive communication I'm capable of. I usually wasn't so callous, but like I told Trevor, today is not my day.

He lifts his almost empty glass in the air towards me and then swallows down the rest of the liquor. Almost without hesitation, the bartender scurries over and offers him another drink in a fresh glass.

I raise my martini back to him and take another long sip. "The fucking worst," I mutter almost to myself.

"Swap stories? Wallow without judgment?" he asks with a raised eyebrow and a sexy smirk.

I look down at my phone to check the time. "Might as well since my flight has been delayed for three hours."

He slides off his stool and settles back onto the one closest to me. He leans in, holding out his hand to me. I reach my hand out to meet him, very aware of my grossly sweaty palms. Of course, he smells fantastic. Like a fucking fantasy: expensive and refined with notes of sandalwood and oud.

"Vincent Crawford." He shakes my hand firmly as he raises an eyebrow as if to ask my name in return. A current of electricity travels through my body at his touch. Yup, this is the kind of guy who could completely fuck up your life in two-point-five seconds.

"Alison. Alison Ryder," I say, trying not to stare at his full lips.

"Well, since I offered, I'll go first, then you can decide how much you want to share to make me feel better about whining to a stranger." I laugh a little as he moves the glass back and forth between his hands.

"So, I work for a luxury hotel chain based in Chicago. I am currently in the middle of an acquisition in London and another possible one in Toronto. I am actually on my way to Canada now to meet with the current owner of a hotel there, after which I go home for a week or so, then off to London."

I sip my martini as he continues to expound on his travel plans that will be taking place over the next several months and the time it took to get everything organized.

"So anyway, my executive assistant that helped me plan all of these trips was supposed to travel with me, but today, she up and quit because she fell in love and eloped. This caused a chain reaction of events: since she quit, she didn't confirm my travel plans with my private jet, so they ended up submitting flight plans too late to get approved. Now I'm stuck on a commercial flight, which is getting me into Toronto at an ungodly hour, if it departs in the next hour as scheduled and causing me to miss my initial meeting."

I can see he is getting more and more exasperated, although he's barely changed his cadence or demeanor, remaining calm. He's clearly a meticulous and punctual man who doesn't appreciate being late or having his schedule interrupted.

"Jesus, that sounds like a nightmare. I'm sorry. Is your boss at least being understanding about everything?"

He stares into his glass as he swirls the remaining liquor around before downing it. He shakes his head as he swallows. "Sorry, I forgot to mention, I am the boss. I own the company, so it's just frustrating me more than normal that I am now stuck with no assistant to help me as I manage this possible new acquisition. Normally I'm very easy going, I like to think of myself as laid back, but when it comes to the reputation of my company, I can't help but get a little riled up."

"Hey, I get it. I'm very type-A, so I can imagine how frustrating that would be. When's your next trip after this one? Do you have time to hire an executive assistant before then?"

"I'll be in Toronto for four days, so I'll have about ten days to interview and hire a new EA before flying to London for other business. I sent an email to my vice president's secretary to see if she can help me get the ball rolling. The hard part will be finding someone willing to travel all over the damn globe almost immediately after starting. I prefer to build trust with someone before exposing them to such confidential information and putting those kinds of demands on them. Anyway, at this point, I'm just complaining. Your turn," he says, raising his empty glass to me.

"Well, we did agree we would wallow without judgment." I finish the rest of my martini before launching into my story.

"Funny enough, I am also from Chicago. Well—originally I'm from North Dakota, but I moved to Chicago for college and stayed because, well, it's Chicago!" I'm rambling like a ditzy high schooler, my hands gesturing a bit wildly. I don't know if it's the alcohol, the frazzled state of my nerves, or the sexy stranger that has me acting completely out of character.

"I'm an associate at a very prestigious design firm, Madeline Dwyer Designs...I did my internship there through undergrad and then worked my way up from junior associate to associate...working towards senior and then partner, or maybe owning my own firm someday. My fiancé is a senior associate at a big law firm, about to be made partner. He and I have been together for six years. I met him when I was still in school. I was working through my internship and went to a local bar where the lawyers from his firm frequented. He was a junior associate at the time." I let out a big breath to gather my thoughts and try to slow the two martinis from going straight to my head.

"So anyway, he proposed seven months ago, and we set a date for June of next year. Recently, his firm's Dallas office took on a huge class-action lawsuit, and they needed some help so Brian, my fiancé, volunteered to go. He took a few of the interns with him, and they've been there for a few weeks. My boss asked me if I wanted time off to fly down and see him for a few days, and naturally, I jumped at the opportunity. I missed him and hadn't seen him for so long." I feel myself rambling, so I take another deep breath to steady myself.

"So, short story long, I showed up to his hotel last night to surprise him and found him with one of his interns. He had her bent over the desk in the room and was giving her the business end of a deposition, if you know what I mean!" I snort, half at my punny joke and half to emphasize my point.

Vincent smirks a little at the comment. "I did not go to law school, but I can deduce what that statement means."

"I didn't even say a word to him; I just turned around and left the room. I was shocked and didn't even know what to do. He followed me and tried apologizing and giving every excuse in the book from 'it's not what you think,' to 'it's your fault because you haven't come to visit me here.' I just took the ring off and handed it back to him, er—maybe I threw it at him; I can't recall. We live together, so that's another nightmare I have to figure out when I get back. I haven't told my sister or my boss."

Shock registers on his otherwise passive face. "You win. Not that it's a competition, that sounds rude, but fuck. You've had one shitty day. Not to pry, but did you suspect anything?"

"I wouldn't say I suspected infidelity but…the truth is I was settling. I think I was aware of that; I just didn't want to admit it. When I met Brian, things were great; we were young and in love and all that. But now…" I feel my words slurring together. I am wildly out of character at this point. Miss Type-A, always in control and uptight, is letting it all out to a complete stranger. I rub my hand over my face, most likely smearing my makeup. "I mean, I still love him…it just fucking sucks to put your trust and faith in someone and have this entire life planned out and they just throw you away for someone that 'didn't mean anything.'" I make sure to use dramatic air quotes to emphasize my point.

I look over at him as I shrug my shoulders in shame. He's unsure of what to say, but his eyes are sympathetic to my situation.

"I feel like a privileged asshole complaining about this stuff. I'm sorry."

He reaches out and brushes a stray section of hair behind my ear. It startles me, and I'm sure the emotion shows on my face as he pulls his hand back quickly.

"I'm sorry, I hate seeing a beautiful woman cry." His eyes drop to my lips briefly before he turns back to face his drink.

"Well, Alison, you do have a right to be unhappy about where your life is going; privileged or not, we all deserve happiness. The important thing is, if you are unhappy, you have to be willing to be uncomfortable to change it. Otherwise, you'll be stuck in the same situation complaining about the same things over and over. The big question now is, what are you going to do?"

I let out a deep sigh as I look up toward the ceiling. "I don't have a fucking clue, Vincent." I can feel my phone vibrate in my pocket again as the bartender sends me over another dirty vodka martini. I nod a thank you and reach into my pocket. "Finally! My flight is scheduled to depart in the next thirty-five minutes; looks like my delay was cut short. My section should be boarding soon."

Vincent checks his watch and then pulls out his phone. "Lucky you. Looks like my flight is still delayed with no scheduled departure."

I throw a few bills on the bar top and stand up to gather my things. "Thanks for being my airport therapist. It was nice to talk so freely to a complete stranger, admitting things that I haven't even said aloud to myself."

"Happy to listen. It was lovely meeting you, Alison Ryder."

He gives me a crooked smile as he reaches into his pocket again and pulls out his business card.

"In case you need someone to drink an overpriced martini and have another therapy session with when you get back to Chicago." I smile and take the card from him; our fingertips briefly touch, sending a current through my body. Just as I turn to walk away, he pipes back up.

"Oh, and if you're looking to completely uproot your life, I'm looking for an assistant." I laugh, unsure if he's serious, but a little intrigued at the idea. I won't lie: the thought of jet setting around Europe for several weeks on someone else's dime sounds like a dream job…especially if it means spending time with him every day.

"Thanks again, Vincent. It was great meeting you. I hope you get everything sorted and can find a replacement assistant soon. Best of luck on the acquisition!"

I grab my suitcase and make my way toward my gate. I know I just met the man, but weirdly I feel a little sad walking away from him. A small part also questions if he really just hit on me after telling him I found my fiancé cheating. The thought of Brian makes my stomach churn…I feel like a piece of shit too. I'm still coasting on the realization that my six-year relationship is over and my heart's broken while I'm fantasizing about a complete stranger.

I am technically now homeless and single…I just need to get on my flight and let my thoughts marinate in the vodka now sloshing around my brain.

GRAB BUSINESS & PLEASURE HERE!

READ THE REST OF THE
SERIES HERE

Business & Pleasure: Castille Hotel Series Book 1
Baby Mistake: Castille Hotel Series Book 2
Fake It: Castille Hotel Series Book 3

WANT A FREE BOOK FROM ME?

How the hell am I supposed to focus when all I can think about is tearing that tight suit from his tempting body!

What's even worse?
He forgot to mention, he's my boss.

SIGN UP HERE

ALSO BY ALEXIS WINTER

Men of Rocky Mountain Series

Claiming Her Forever

A Second Chance at Forever

Always Be My Forever

Only for Forever

Waiting for Forever

Billionaire Stand-Alone

Dirty Little Secret

Make Her Mine Series

My Best Friend's Brother

Billionaire With Benefits

My Boss's Sister

My Best Friend's Ex

Best Friend's Baby

Love You Forever Series

The Wrong Brother

Marrying My Best Friend's BFF

Breaking Up with My Boss

My Accidental Forever

The F It List

The Baby Fling

Grand Lake Colorado Series

A Complete Small-Town Contemporary Romance Collection

Never Too Late Series

Never Too Late: A Complete Contemporary Romance Second Chance Collection

Slade Brothers Series

Billionaire's Unexpected Bride

Off Limits Daddy

Baby Secret

Loves me NOT

Best Friend's Sister

Castille Hotel Series

Hate That I Love You

Business & Pleasure

Baby Mistake

Fake It

South Side Boys Series

Bad Boy Protector-Book 1

Fake Boyfriend-Book 2

Brother-in-law's Baby-Book 3

Bad Boy's Baby-Book 4

Mountain Ridge Series

Just Friends: Mountain Ridge Book 1

Protect Me: Mountain Ridge Book 2

Baby Shock: Mountain Ridge Book 3

ALL BOOKS CAN BE READ AS STAND-ALONE READS WITHIN THESE SERIES

ABOUT THE AUTHOR

Alexis Winter is a contemporary romance author who loves to share her steamy stories with the world. She specializes in billionaires, alpha males and the women they love.

If you love to curl up with a good romance book you will certainly enjoy her work. Whether it's a story about an innocent young woman learning about the world or a sassy and fierce heroine who knows what she wants you,'re sure to enjoy the happily ever afters she provides.

When Alexis isn't writing away furiously, you can find her exploring the Rocky Mountains, traveling, enjoying a glass of wine or petting a cat.

You can find her books on Amazon or at https://www.alexiswinterauthor.com/

Follow Alexis Winter below for access to advanced copies of upcoming releases, fun giveaways and exclusive deals!

Made in the USA
Monee, IL
20 May 2022

96759362R00059